THE SIZE OF THE WORLD

Ivana Skye

THE SIZE OF THE WORLD

Published by Eta Carinae Press in 2016

ISBN: 978-0-9978544-9-7

To those who said this shouldn't be written.

1

THE SKY above me does not seem like a sky. It absorbs the colors of the ground beneath, which are not the colors I know: not green, not grey, not brown. Instead its colors are orange; its colors are red.

And instead of stone, there is sand.

And the clouds are only wisps.

And the ground seems almost like water, though it is solid.

The air is warm to breathe, and sweet. I take off my cloak and tie it around my waist. It and the shirt and pants beneath are my only possessions. My boat was hours-ago discarded — useless, the next Sea so far away.

I have only crossed the First Sea. There are six more.

I have crossed the First Sea, and I see no food, no water, no people. So I must walk.

And when I look down, the sun too bright, I see the ripples my footsteps leave.

I BECOME thirsty so I lean to the ground, to the ripples above the sand. I aim to touch the water, to hold it in my hand. I cannot. It is solid, evading my grasp.

The sun is bright. High in the sky. Night is far off.

I lie down and place my tongue against the ground. The water is still solid. Still evading my touch.

Yet, I feel refreshed.

The taste is like oranges.

My footsteps seem far as I walk. Time, even farther. My only direction is Outward. Away from the First Kingdom. Toward the Third. And, eventually, the Seventh. Then, the Darkness.

The shadows cast by the dunes are lengthening. I walk through one of these shadows, seeing a sky half-white with sun but feeling only a chill.

The wind tastes like roses.

My mind drifts into the varying colors of the sand, into the clearing sky.

AND IT is night.

The colors of the sand faded into dark. The stars shining. I have passed two more dunes. And the brightest of stars is beginning to rise.

And the wind is stronger now, strong as a river.

NEAR DAWN the wind fades, taking with it the taste of jasmine and honey. No shadows are cast, no light is stronger than any other.

It is quiet, and I close my eyes.

In my dreams I walk, ripples following me. I do the same as I wake, and I cannot mark the moment when I open my eyes.

The silence is broken by the cry of a bird. It is white, and I do not recognize it.

I turn to follow.

I DO NOT walk in straight lines. Instead, I walk around the dunes.

I have long lost the bird.

I am alone.

I IMAGINE:

I will find other people, I will find a city, I will find a king. I have been told these things exist here. When I have looked Outward, toward the Darkness, I have seen structures. Perhaps rising from this land. Perhaps not.

But I will be greeted.

And when I am greeted and respond with my name, it will not be the name I was born to.

I know this now. I plan this. I will speak, and from my voice will come a name. Talarisa. Zhenfera. Otala. None of these.

THE SUN is setting. Wisps of clouds catch the light, make it pink.

The dunes are sparse here. No footprints, not even my own. No voices, not even that of birds. I am all that is here.

But then the wind blows again and carries the scent of oranges.

I HEAR breath.

The stars are bright in the sky, and not even the wind can mask what I hear. Two exhalations, out of rhythm. Two inhalations, out of rhythm.

There is another here.

I walk to the sound. A figure walks also, from behind a dune. This dune pure white in the starlight. But where her shadow falls the sand turns orange.

The other rushes, but I walk faster. Until I see her clearly. A woman wearing a straw hat, loose pants. Her skin the color of the sparkling of sunlit sand. Her hair the color of the shadow of a dune. Across her face, marks like the stars, but dark instead of bright.

"This is not your Land," she says. I am close enough to catch her smile.

I shake my head.

"It is mine," she continues. Her words are as different from mine as stone from sand. Yet, I understand.

She steps closer. "And who are you?"

I am not sure how to respond, and so do not.

"That's alright," she says. "Anyway — would you like me to take you to my city?"

MY GUIDE extends her hand. I take it, and it is as smooth as the solidity of the water.

"This way," she says.

So I follow her as she begins the ascent of a dune. The water gives way below my feet as I follow her, as if making steps.

"Easy, isn't it?" my guide says. "Don't worry. It'll get even easier."

THE STARS are bright in my guide's face when we reach the top. She sits down, and I do the same.

"Lie down," she says.

I do.

Her hands against me, pushing me.

I roll down the dune. It is smooth against me and when it touches my mouth, it tastes like lemon. Then grapefruit. Then champagne.

Sight blurs, as do touch and taste.

There is wind against me and also water, and I am not sure which direction each come from.

And I come to a stop at the base of the dune.

Then my guide, a few feet left of me. Smiling, motioning me up, her hair seeming almost wet.

WE CROSS all dunes like this, and travel is much faster.

The sun is risen, a hand-length above the nearest dune, when I see a silver structure, nestled between three huge dunes.

"That's it," my guide says, "the wall to my city." And readjusts her hat.

THE CITY wall glistens and steams. As I draw closer, I understand why. It is made of ice and is evaporating where the sun touches it.

I stare, but my guide walks right up to it. "City of the White Center," she whispers, her mouth so close to the ice. A crack forms and the ice slides open, smooth as glass.

As we walk through this opening, through this gate, I touch the wall. It is strangely hot.

AND WE step into the city. Here beneath the water of the ground are rounded pebbles, not sand. There are buildings: rocks which reach out from the ground, also coated in water, like a waterfall.

The colors here are red, like some of the sands I've seen. My guide has said the center is white.

And all around people move, but they do not look directly before them the way my people do. Instead they glance, and at times they stop mid-stride. They move like a windstorm.

"But *you* need rest," my guide says.

So I follow her, eyes focused on her footsteps.

THE COLORS of the sand below the water below my feet become orange and then yellow, then fainter, nearly white. The color of clouds in the sun.

We walk toward a rock, a building, tall though not very wide. The top of the rock is a bright, sun-bleached white. The steps to the door are carved in.

I cannot tell how my guide opens the door, but she does and we walk inside.

There is light. Sections of the rock now *are* waterfalls, the rock removed. Windows.

The next set of stairs is also carved in, on the internal walls surrounding the lower room. The upper room it leads to has a bed, and my guide motions me into it.

I sleep.

AND DREAM of butterflies landing on ivy growing on grey stone walls.

2

I WAKE TO afternoon light filtered through water and the simple sounds of motion from below me.

So I walk down the steps. I find a feast. Fruits and dried flowers arrayed across a stone table. Though this is the first stone I have seen free of the solid water here.

I sit across from her and eat with a grateful smile.

And then.

I SAY FASTER than I can realize: "Theia. My name is Theia."

"Theia," she says, grinning. "That is a good name. It tastes like ivy in my mouth."

"Who are you?" I ask.

"I am Tellus," she says, "if you wish."

"If I wish?"

"Tell me," she whispers, "have you ever met someone with only one name?"

"Yes," I say. There is nothing in common between my Kingdom and hers.

"In this Land," she proclaims, "you never will."

"THEIA," TELLUS says. My head turns, though I was not born with this name. "Why is it you're here?"

"I am seeking."

"What are you seeking?"

"Everything, perhaps."

IT IS HALF a day before we speak again, although every time Tellus glances at me it is with a smile. It is dawn, though she has already woken. I say, "I am rested now and should leave."

This time she does not smile. "You've barely seen this city!" She says, "At least meet with the king before you leave."

"The ruler of a Kingdom is a busy man."

"Not a Kingdom," Tellus says, "just a city of many names in a land of desert."

"I know," I say.

"No, you don't."

SO MY GUIDE brings me to the center of the city. As we approach, the sands grow whiter, sparkle more in the light. And even before we are there the center is clear, taller than all the other buildings in the city, surrounded by a waterfall.

"You say we can enter?" I ask.

"My mother works here," Tellus says. "My father too, sometimes, when he isn't working elsewhere. The life of a courtesan is chaotic."

"And your mother?"

"A jester. The top one, actually. But come on already, let's enter." And so she simply reaches out her hand and opens the door.

THE PALACE GLISTENS on the inside as well, with some windows large enough to give diffuse light to entire halls, and others much smaller, directing sunbeams into carefully placed prisms that paint this castle of white rock with color. Except for orange; that color is missing.

Then, I look down. Cast on the ground, as well as on my hands, is the color orange — sent here by smaller, precise prisms to form a path. Which we are following.

"This leads to the King?" I ask.

"It does. Dramatic, isn't it?"

THE DOOR TO the King's throne seems made of pearl, and this Tellus cannot open. Instead, she knocks.

"We'll be let in," she says. And the doors open.

Tellus bows in the same motion that brings her forward into the King's sight. It is a shallow bow, but seems enough. I follow her lead.

"Welcome, dear," he announces, perhaps having known Tellus all her life. "Who is this that is with you?"

"Vena," I say, and stand.

"You are the color of stone under a stream and, though you follow this one's example well," he says and looks at Tellus, then back to me, "you are from the First Land. None from there have entered the Second Land since ... perhaps never."

"Yet you know where I am from. Though it is a Kingdom, and not a Land."

"Your mountain at the center of the First Sea is not hard to notice."

I smile and quickly bow my head.

THE SIZE OF THE WORLD

"SO, VENA, as you have introduced yourself," the King says, "why did you do what has never been done and cross the First Sea?"

"Because I intend to cross the Second Sea, and the Third, and the Fourth, and the Fifth, and the Sixth, and the Seventh into the Darkness itself."

"All this for knowledge?" he asks.

"No," I say.

"And power?"

"No," I say.

"For another reason?"

"Perhaps," I say.

"Not badly spoken," he says, "though not well spoken either." He pauses. "I trust you will appreciate the Festival tomorrow. I am willing to pay for whatever expenses you'll spend then."

"YOU KNEW he would offer," I say — I who had intended to already have left this city.

"Among other things," Tellus says.

We have left the palace, and I am following Tellus in her stroll on paths underneath the shade of buildings.

"In fact," she says, quietly, "now I also know where you intend to go."

We stop near a building midway between the center and edge of the city. It is mostly a pale orange but has been splattered with several colors of paint. Voices echo from inside, and even outside it is surrounded by people. We stand behind the furthest person from the building.

"The Festival starts at dawn," Tellus says. "But everyone gets ready before then."

She looks at my hair, the texture of moss and in a short braid that stops just below my neck. "Want to cut that off?"

THE SIZE OF THE WORLD

"OF COURSE, the Festival has other names," Tellus says when we are a little further in line to enter the building. "The Year's Dawn, The Time of New Names, The Day of Change."

"Why will you cut my hair?" I ask.

"Oh, 'people flow like water between one moment and the next.' It's just a quote, but it's true. Today, we alter our bodies to match."

She opens her left palm to me and points to a scar shaped like the sun with rays coming out. "That's from a few years ago. This year . . . well, you'll see." She pauses. "It is up to you though. Doesn't have to be your hair. Or anything. But you're here now, and the King's paying for it. This shop has anything you ask for."

I nod and wish for summer meadows beneath my feet, for the sight of solid grey stone.

IT IS AFTERNOON when we walk back to my guide's house to eat fruit and sleep in preparation for the dawn.

My hair is now only an inch from my head, although an orange string has been threaded through it on the right side. My lower arms and neck are painted in white patterns, which I hear are not permanent. I also have new clothes: a comfortable dress that looks white from a distance but glistens green when one comes close, and a light tan cloak to go over it when it is cold. There is also a way to attach the lower part of the dress to the cloak, and there are pants I wear underneath, not currently visible.

Tellus' hair is now streaked red and orange to add to its natural yellow. The colors of the desert sands. She wears a bright red dress wrapped with an orange sash. And still wears her hat.

"Orange, huh?" She points to the strand in my hair with a smirk.

"Yes. And you change this little after all today?" I ask.

"It's more than my hair, trust me." And that is all she says.

THE SIZE OF THE WORLD

THE TWILIGHT before the sunrise is loud, and it is when we wake. "Quick," Tellus says."We'll need to get to the market. It's the best place for the Festival."

"Alright," I say, yawning.

"You won't regret it, Theia!"

And she rushes out the door, motioning me to follow. I do so, as I have before.

This time, I notice that starlight reflects differently off pebbles than it does off sand. And though the city has little smell or taste, I breathe deeply, and it is like drinking water.

THERE IS A MAN with metal in his nose. And there is a woman with feet dyed black. And there is a girl whose hair spikes upward. And there is a boy with sparkles under his eyes. And this one's hair is shaved, with metal in his eyebrows — but maybe hers, because despite the harshness of this person's face, they wear a dress. This is not the only person whose gender is difficult to discern.

"Some once seen as men now show themselves as women, as I did years ago," Tellus says to me. "And some once seen as women now show themselves as men, and some show themselves as other types. And some who were bare are covered with piercings, and some had piercings removed, and everyone's hair is a different color …"

"I can see."

"So can I," Tellus says. "Better than you, because I see that ladder over there to the top of a building where we can watch the sunrise. Come on!" She smiles.

"This is a good day for your kingdom," I note, as I look around the people here. "You're not the only one who's grinning."

THE TOP OF the building is quiet for a while, but as soon as we climb the ladder, others notice and follow. Still, we sit in the highest place available and face the direction of the sunrise.

Already the sky is more light than dark, and some wisps of cloud have turned pink against the near-green of the lower part of the sky. We look Inward, where my mountain is visible in the distance, though it seems small from here.

The sun becomes visible so quickly that it would have been hard to pinpoint the exact moment it begins rising in full, if it weren't for the fact that every person in the city cheers just now. And perhaps people in other cities in this Land cheer as well.

As the light crosses the sky, turning it blue, the color of each person here is revealed. Tellus' hair glows in the light, and she is not alone. Many people's skin, adorned with oil or glitter, shines now. And what was already visible brightens.

"YOU LIKED THE sunrise," Tellus says, "but it's morning now and the food's even better!"

So we climb down the ladder, and it is instantaneous — merchants are showing us their flavored breads, fruit samples are shoved towards us, and there are more scents than in all the desert.

I smile as I chew on a grape; Tellus buys two slices of hibiscus-lemon bread and gives one to me. I point at a banana-papaya-orange cake, and she buys two slices of that too. I eat a pink orange someone gives me, and we try grapefruit in every color. We drink glasses of wine with jasmine-honey bread.

Confetti falls from every direction, and it is too loud to talk. So Tellus just smiles at me and grabs my hand. I grab back.

IT IS PERHAPS two hours past noon when Tellus falls asleep in the heat of the sun.

I know the direction to the gate; all I have to do is follow the pebbles as they grow more red.

I walk. The gate opens for me. I go through it.

Then I feel something on my hand and turn around. Tellus is holding it with a sigh and a pout.

"I knew it," she says.

"You-"

"Followed you, of course." She sighs again. "I thought you were having fun."

"I was," I say, "but I am going toward the Second Sea."

"Well," Tellus says, "so am I."

3

"AND NOW I ask you," I say, "why is it you're going where I'm going?"

"No one leaves the First Kingdom and no one crosses all seven Seas and no one visits the Darkness," she says.

I nod. "Does it matter, which direction we approach the Third Sea from?"

"It might, if we have a boat. Unless you were hoping to swim?"

"Perhaps we can buy the materials from a city closer to the water."

"Then yes, it does matter how we get there. There's only one city built next to the water. Thankfully, it's not far Clockwise from here."

"You are my guide again," I say.

"See? You would've drowned without me."

THE SIZE OF THE WORLD

"WHAT WAS your Kingdom like?" Tellus asks me.

"You can see it from yours," I say.

"But I can't see the ivy growing in it."

I sigh. "It is a mountain with many rivers. The lower part is forests and rice fields; the upper part where trees cannot grow is meadows and the palace."

"Boring enough to leave, huh?"

I look into her eyes. "No." Then I look away. "Perhaps."

Tellus does not speak again for some time.

WE JOURNEY as we have journeyed before, with little regard to time of day, resting when we need to and walking all other times. We walk up dunes and roll down them. Sometimes Tellus laughs during this. Sometimes I do.

"It's tiring, trying to coax out everyone's names in the Ice-Walled City, playing all those political games," Tellus says. "I like it better out here."

"Have you been where we're going?"

"The City by the Sea? Once. By accident. Let's hope the queen there forgot, or maybe died."

I look at her with my eyebrows raised.

"I'll tell you if you tell me why you left," she says.

"Sounds like you're still playing political games," I say.

WE ARE ABLE to see the Sea before we've gone Clockwise enough to reach the city. It is stark in its blue and reflective whites, and I cannot see the Kingdom or Land beyond it. I breathe deeply. "I should tell you why I left," I say, "so that you can let me know if we can safely leave here."

Tellus smiles to herself. "Go ahead."

"I left because I was already the girl who tore wings from butterflies to reveal how much they look like ants. I looked and the others did not, just as they did not look when I left."

Silence passes until Tellus accepts that is what I have to say.

"I was young when I wandered here the first time," she says, "and I may have pulled some levers I shouldn't have, and I *may* have destroyed the gates to what is now called the Gateless City."

"Will they do business with us?" I ask.

"Don't worry," Tellus says, "any of my names will fetch a great price. We can probably buy a boat outright instead of making one."

"So you didn't really want the Queen to forget. This was another game."

"Really? So impressive of you to notice."

I DISCOVER THE Gateless City is naturally walled by mostly yellowish dunes, except for one break between them, where the gate once was.

Tellus walks directly through. I follow, eyes fixed ahead as those on the outskirts of the City begin whispering.

"Are you that recognizable?" I ask Tellus.

"Same hat," she replies.

THEN I HEAR the words and the whispers aren't about her. They're about me.

"Who's that woman with skin the color of river stone?"

"I hear people from the First Land look like that."

"I hear the First Land is really called the First Kingdom."

"Who cares, I thought no one *left* it!"

"Why is she here with that other woman?"

"Wait, I think I recognize that hat!"

"You said that the *last* five times someone entered the City!"

"But this time it is the hat!"

"Calm down, old woman, and start paying attention to the First Kingdom woman in our midst!"

I walk in front of Tellus and address the growing crowd. "If you're so impressed, tell me where I can buy a boat."

"But who are you?" "Are you really from there?" "Boats don't grow on dunes." "Hardly anyone crosses the Seas."

"I cross the Seas," I say, my voice hard as stone.

A girl jostles her way to the front of the crowd and says in a timid voice, "That way. Thirteen buildings down. The man there owns a boat."

TELLUS KNOCKS on the door. "I really did think they'd recognize me," she says.

Before I have time to respond, the door opens. The man who greets us is old, his hair as white as the pebbles in the center of Tellus' city.

"Hello," I say.

"Any chance we can buy your boat?" Tellus asks.

He looks at us suspiciously and says, "I'm not going to go selling my boat for just anything."

"Even if I have any name you'd need of the girl who broke the city gates?"

"Hmm. That is different. How did you come about that information, if you don't mind my asking?"

"Could be I am her," Tellus says, with a sheepish smile.

"I'll still sell it for no less than a third of your names," he says.

"Deal."

Tellus mouths the words *told you* to me before she goes inside his house to give him names I am not meant to hear.

OUR AUDIENCE is even larger when we leave the City by the Sea carrying a boat. People point openly, whisper too loudly — "They're really doing it!" "What's an upstanding Second Lander like her doing crossing the Seas?" "Where'd they get the boat?" "She isn't really from the First Land, right?" — and follow us a few paces outside the missing gates.

We leave them behind and hear only the crash of the waves.

OVER THE sound of the waves, Tellus speaks, looking directly into my eyes. "You made an impression."

I nod.

She gives a small smile, her head tilted away. "Tell me to stop, if you need," she says.

Before I can ask a question she steps to me, her feet touching mine, her head now approaching mine, and —

Her lips touching mine.

And I should think, I should decide what I need, and she tastes like oranges, she tastes like oranges, and I am pulling forward not away, and I taste metal on her tongue, and it tastes sharp, like the sharpness as she bites me —

She is the one to pull away, and I do not know what expression she sees on my face.

She sticks out her tongue and points to it, and I see the metal piercing running through it, shaped like ivy on the top. "I told you I changed more than my hair," she says. I do not respond and she asks, "You- liked it?"

"How," I manage to say, "did you plan … ivy …?"

"I told you your name tasted like it and guessed *you* would too. Also guessed I'd get the chance to find out."

I have heard of faces turning red like flowers, so I turn away, so that she doesn't see.

But I whisper: "Yes, I … think I did like it."

WE WALK, and I try not to look to Tellus. I cannot tell if I'm smiling. And as we approach the Sea, the sound of waves gets stronger. We cross between the dunes, and I see it, the water the same grey-blue as the First Sea.

Some of the sand here begins to stick to my feet, as if the proximity of saltwater frees it. Tellus yelps when she notices this. I laugh and dare turn to her.

"The Land of solid water is over," I tell her, "tell me if *you* need to stop."

"I . . . I don't," she says.

WE PLACE the boat on the sand near where the waves begin and sit, me before Tellus. I give her one of the two oars, and we push out into the Second Sea.

4

WE ARE ON the Sea, and I am steering the boat with the taste of orange still in my mouth, but Tellus is silent behind me. I look to her, and she is looking elsewhere, Inward, back to her home.

"You don't need to follow me," I say. "You could return."

"But I won't," she says.

Still she looks back, and the taste of her begins to evaporate the way the droplets of the Sea on my skin are evaporating now.

AND ALL AROUND us is blue, the Sea hinting at green and the sky open wide, hinting at nothing at all. There are waves and there is movement, but it is easy to direct the boat Outward, away from the still-visible dunes of the Second Land.

Toward a darker sky.

Hardly darker at all. Perhaps impossible to notice, if one did not know the Darkness was in that direction.

But all know.

So we row on this Sea, away from the Second Land, away from the First Kingdom, away from what was my home.

Away from Tellus' Land, too.

"WHEN YOU stepped on my Land," Tellus begins.

"I stepped again," I say. "And again. Each step moving me forward."

She nods and turns now Outward, where the Third Kingdom will be. "Why can't we see it?" she asks.

"Perhaps we *are* looking at it."

"Is it just the Sea, then? The Sea forever?"

"There *are* Seven Kingdoms; no one disbelieves that."

"Then what is it, the Third Land?"

"I do not know."

MY THOUGHTS can barely take hold in this place where no one can live. So I do not recognize the passage of time until Tellus says: "Theia?"

"Yes?"

She smiles and shakes her head. "You do, by the way," she says. "You do taste like ivy."

5

AND THE Second Sea ends, slowly and yet still abruptly, for I can see no land. The boat simply stops, no longer on water.

Tellus says nothing, and perhaps she is frightened. She looks to me.

I dismount the boat. Slowly, one foot then the other, in order not to fall.

But I do not fall. I seem to stand on nothing more than a twist of colored light, a trick of the sun — but I stand.

TELLUS STANDS behind me and asks, "Is this still the Sea?"

"No," I answer.

I walk, and she asks: "We're leaving the boat?"

"The Fourth Sea is too far. We'll find another, as I found one in your Land."

She looks between me and the boat, and she follows me.

Around us, all is sky reflected on sea, though there is no longer a sea; perhaps the sky reflects the sky. The sunlight falls directly on our skin, yet is only warm and not hot. To our sides, above, and below is mostly blue, the shades shifting slightly between each cloud.

What we stand on is faint, a green light difficult to see against the day. Yet in some directions, I seem to see stars.

WE ARE CAREFUL, as it seems easy to fall. If I hold up my hand, I find stars in between each finger; the wind sounds like whispering.

Tellus whispers also, and I look to her.

"My names," she explains, "in case they change."

The sky is darkening and the clouds are pink as they move across the sky. Also now visible against this open sky are strands of colored light, of every color, like the one we walk on now. They are pathways, and they are everywhere.

The wind's whispering grows louder and, though footsteps here make no sound, it appears we are approaching another person.

THE FOOTSTEPS draw closer, and the man who walks to us through a cloud is pale as starlight. He looks at us as he walks by and does not stop until he is three paces behind us. Then he turns around and asks, "Who are you?"

"Travelers," I say.

"Aren't we all?" he responds. Then, a pout and: "I was honestly curious, who you are."

"Lileta," Tellus speaks quickly, and then quieter, "from the Second Land."

"Fascinating!" The man responds. "And you?"

"I am from the First Kingdom," I say. "My name is Theia."

Tellus looks to me, and I cannot read her expression; there is too much there to possibly read.

"My name is Ávelé," the man says. "It is very nice to meet both of you. And very unusual. May I treat you to a meal?"

TELLUS NEITHER looks at me nor talks as we follow Ávelé. Even the shimmer we walk on begins to split between us. In the middle of this ground now I can see clearly the deep blue of the early evening sky beneath us, untainted by the green of our path.

And on Tellus' side of the path, the green is becoming more yellow, nearly a distinct color from mine.

All that is not silent is footsteps, but even footsteps are quiet on this ground. Like walking on silk. Even my own, I can only hear when I try to.

So I let the sky darken in silence.

IT IS FULL nighttime when we reach a convergence of paths — a convergence of colors — and Ávelé motions us to sit, floating in the stars. The ground beneath us seems to swirl, and it is rainbows not displayed in rainbow order, coloring the sky whenever we look down.

Ávelé takes out a pouch from his cloak and, from there, a glow almost too bright to look at. Brighter than the ground.

A moment of waiting passes before I realize this is the meal, so I take one of the pieces in the pouch set before us. It melts in my mouth and is as strong as pepper, but fresh and bright rather than spicy.

I look to Tellus, and she looks away, but she has eaten a piece.

"SO …" ÁVELÉ says.

"It is good," I say.

"Have you ever seen anything like it?" he asks, his eyes near sparkling.

"No," I say.

"Want to guess what it is?"

Tellus shakes her head and looks into the distance.

"I do not know what it is," I say.

"It's a fallen star. And," he adds, "you should let her go. Lileta."

I feel my face redden. "Let her-?"

"Whoa," he says, "just some advice. I'm sure you'll see her again! Just — let her go."

Silently, at that moment, the path rends entirely in two, separating the crossroads as well.

I DREAM of names; I dream of fear. Even within my dreams, I cannot remember them.

I wake to a shaking that dies down as I face the sun, Ávelé no longer here. Alone again.

I DO NOT know where I go as I walk, and I cannot tell direction. Clockwise? Counterclockwise? Inward? Outward? There is only sky, and sky bounded only by sky provides no reference.

The sun is directly above, if the blue is not confusing my sense of *up,* but the light is shifting somehow.

Still I continue this path, though it is so bright I must close my eyes against the sun.

"HELLO AGAIN." Ávelé.

"Do you know which direction is Outward?" I ask.

"Ah, that. Uh," he starts, "not really. Though if you can keep yourself going straight, you'll probably find the Third Sea. Eventually."

I nod.

Then: "Does the sun always set and rise on the same path, each day?" I ask.

"Seems so," Ávelé says.

"Alright," I say, "I use the sun."

IT IS NOT easy. I go in the direction of morning, which makes afternoon travel difficult and nighttime travel impossible. The wisps of light and cloud, the patterns of sky, the occasional taste of starlight in my mouth, all blend together.

All I know is my footsteps; I am not even certain of my direction.

In hopes of the Third Sea. In hopes of the Fourth Kingdom. And-

Ahead. I see her. Lileta. Tellus.

6

"YOU TOLD him your name was Theia," she says.

"Yes," I say.

"That was the name you gave me. That was the part of yourself you showed *me*." Her teeth are gritted, her eyes are narrow.

"Yes," I say.

"And who is he?" she asks.

"That is the wrong question," I say. "The question is who I am. The answer is that I am Theia."

"You were also Vena, and whatever name you were born with-"

"But Theia is the name I gave you, the first name of this journey, a name that tastes like the ivy of my home but sounds like where I have not yet gone. It was the right name to give, because it is who I am. And in this place it seemed I was allotted only one name."

"How could you even tell?" she asks, her voice so quiet it is almost still.

"At least it seemed that way enough in the half second before I responded, and I was not wrong."

SHE LOOKS away and says: "Just make sure to call me what I'm calling myself, when others are listening."

Then we walk forward.

THE CLOUDS Thin ahead of us; the sky seems to melt into the possible sighting of sea. "We are close to the Third Sea," I say.

Tellus walks ahead of me, turns around and stands still, looking me in the eye. Her stance is wide enough to block the path.

Before I can ask a question, she says: "You plan to leave the Third Land so soon?"

A challenge. I try to speak, but-

"You barely lived in my land," she says, quiet, as if wistfully, "and this one, too, you're just passing through quick as you can. You're flying into The Darkness the way a falcon dives from the air — what do you think you're going to learn?"

"I-"

"You said you wanted *everything,* is that true? Is that why you're here?"

"I crossed the First Sea when the flowers were beginning to bloom."

"That isn't relevant-"

"Let me talk." I am speaking slowly, my words are connecting slowly.

But she lets me.

"WHEN I was a child, I said, with a laugh, that I would do this. Cross the Seven Seas, see the Darkness. Though the one in charge of the stream where I grew up heard my words, and looked at me strangely, I made the promise not to her, but to myself.

"And now I fulfill it. The butterflies have lost their wings, and the spores have been torn from the ferns. I've stood at the top of the mountain, the center of my Kingdom, once; there is no need to again."

"I SEEK, Tellus. And also I walk, in lands where walking is all I know. And also I see, I look ahead and see what is there.

"I memorized the colors of the sand, and I am memorizing the color of this sky, but there is nothing I can do beyond what I do.

"No one has seen the Seven Kingdoms, or Lands, or whatever this place calls itself. And no one has seen the Seven Seas. And no one has been inside the Darkness.

"You call me ivy and perhaps I am that persistence, but also I am the persistence of stone.

"How else would I have come this far?"

IT IS a moment before Tellus says, "Maybe there is no other way for you, but there is me. I knew in what you're calling your only name that I would follow you.

"But now you should follow me, and let's find out just what it is that the people here call their Land."

7

I KEEP TELLUS ahead of me, but she looks back at me from time to time, whenever she slows.

The sun disappears from the sky, and the stars collect around us as well as far from us. The paths glow in thousands of colors, mostly greens.

I hear voices around us, and I know it must be more than Ávelé alone. Perhaps not him at all.

IT IS TELLUS who greets the gathering of perhaps thirty people, starlight scattered around them, each pale as the stars the way Ávelé is and each now looking at us. "Hello," Tellus says, "we're obviously not from here, and we can tell you about it, but can we join you?"

Someone nods and motions us to sit, so we walk a bit closer and do. Then the loudness begins, each person asking questions, mostly the same questions, *where* are we from, what are our names?

Tellus answers both: "I'm Vei, and this is Theia. I am from the Second Land, and she is from the First Kingdom."

Speaking begins again from all sides: sounds of awe, confusion, interest.

"And," I say, quietly, yet now they have become quiet enough that I can be heard. "What is the name of this place?"

Now, almost in unison: "The Third Constellation."

WE ARE GIVEN fallen stars to eat. They must be commonplace, though I have not seen any fall.

Tellus is entertaining the crowd: "In my Land, everyone has tens or hundreds of names; the one I introduced myself as is new."

"This is so you can choose your own path, be the person you want to be?" someone asks.

"Something like, though we think of it more as – no one's just one thing." She looks at me then; I am not sure why.

"You said," a boy asks, "that you live in- cities?"

"Yes," Tellus says, "though I must've spent at least half my time in the desert. You haven't seen sand, so I don't know how to explain, but . . . the ground doesn't feel that different on your feet than these paths do."

"Auroras," an old woman says, "these paths are called auroras."

Tellus nods; I am eating the fallen stars. They do not all taste the same, quite — each is bright, but in varying levels. And the taste lasts differing amounts of time: some are stronger earlier in the taste, others grow in flavor.

"BUT THE CITIES, tell me about the cities!" the boy says.

"Well," Tellus says, "they're places where lots of people live. There are these huge rocks- I don't know if there are rocks here, but-"

"I've heard of rocks," the old woman says, "and sand."

Everyone nods assent.

"Okay," Tellus says. "So there are these hollow rocks we live in, that's where we sleep and usually eat. And we talk to each other, *all* the time, trying to learn each others' names."

"We just talk to who we want to," a girl who seems nearly an adult says.

Then I speak: "And what are your names?"

Everyone answers, and I do not keep track. There are names which mean words like Nova and Cerulean, and others that don't, like Vházha and Zleyu, or Secepi and Tephïzu.

Then someone asks to hear of the cities in my Kingdom.

"IT IS NOT cities, but one city, and that city is the Kingdom. All of the great mountain, the circle in the center of the First Sea, is the Kingdom. At the top of the Kingdom, at the top of the mountain, is the King; beneath that are those who help him directly; beneath that is the meadow where the tired rest; then, the forest begins.

"I lived in the forest — most live in the forest. We each do what we are best at and are trained by those who seem to share our aptitude. Those good at shaping tools are the smiths, those who work better with cloth are the seamsters, those who are fast and quiet are the hunters."

"What were you best at?"

"Crossing the Seas."

THE BRIGHTEST of stars has set, and it is deep night, hours before sunrise. The twist of auroras I sit on is purples and pinks. It turns to orange in the distance, where it fades into the sky.

And it is not the only color. Looking at the stars, I notice some are blue, some others red. Occasionally, one seems to sparkle as if green.

And the people here are sleeping, some alone and some in piles, and I am awake. Even Tellus sleeps, though she is close.

It is hard to close my eyes away from what I see.

SO SHE opens her eyes instead.

It is moments before I realize she is looking at me, unmoving. I look to her and back to the sky.

We do not talk.

But she sits closer.

AND THEN the first signal of light is in the air, and she asks me, "What do you see?"

I speak quietly:

"The sky is becoming light now. But the auroras are still brighter, the stars still shine clearly. The black sky is no longer black.

And I sit on a purple aurora, and Tellus looks to me as I talk."

She says: "You see me looking to you, but do you see me thinking about kissing you again?"

THEN I SEE the sky flash with light, the stars obscured now by something which has happened, something which is still happening.

One star has collided into another. And now they are both stardust scattered against the sky, glowing each color and yet mostly white, the stardust thinking to fall back to where the collision occurred, like a broken branch falls to the ground.

I do not know about the Third Constellation, but in the First Kingdom this is called gravity.

So I move to Tellus fast as the light and kiss her.

Only briefly.

She looks to me with surprise, and I smile, and perhaps that is all she sees.

I LIE DOWN the rest of the night, but I do not sleep — my eyes are tracking the stardust in its patterns. Patterns I already know, for I had already seen their gravity.

Perhaps I am not awake, either, for I am surprised when the sun rises and I hear people move all around me, silent but for the soft rustle of fabric. When I sit up, the camp is gone.

"They are with people when they wish and alone when they wish," Tellus says, quietly as if to herself. Then she stands and looks me in the eye. "I can't communicate my desire for companionship or none with the silence or speed they can, but I can guess at what another's thinking, and you — Theia, you're thinking you should leave."

"Perhaps," I say.

"The Fourth Land appeals that much?"

"Perhaps," I say, "and perhaps your names appeal more."

Tellus grins. "What are you willing to- I mean, say- How about-" Tellus shakes her head. "I'm too excited to talk." She takes a breath. "What do you want to buy?"

"How many do you have?"

"That would be telling."

"Five, then."

"Then you'll follow me when I decide to stop and talk to people. From now on." She thinks. "Well, maybe I'll feel like the fee's worn off. Eventually."

"Give me your names."

"SAYEH." AND her eyes open, she looks to the distance, her back is straight. "The one who watches the crowd."

"Senna." And her eyes glisten, she swings her arms back. "The least ambitious girl of the castle."

"Henle." She becomes downcast and quiet. "Who rarely speaks."

"Sesa." She struts forward a step, plays with her hair, looks back to my eyes. "Greatest at idle market conversation."

Then she closes her eyes and whispers, "Ulania." Her posture left open to the wind. "The one the guards see, leaving to the desert."

SO I NOD and I follow her, and where she rushes to is sleep. "We'll travel at night," she says.

So I must close my eyes. And I do.

Inside my dreams, light is still scattering through the sky, and each pinprick is one of her names.

WE WAKE, and it is in between the stars that Tellus explains how the people here make fabric from rays of sunlight. And she reaches and shows reams of it.

I do not know what she has seen away from me. And I do not grasp what she shows me now.

"You said the Third Sea isn't far," she says.

"Explain," I say.

"I may've found out how to make this fabric float on water."

And I look at her, I look to her eyes, and I begin to say, "We arranged-"

"That you follow me, yes," she says. "And you want to move forward, and in this place you not wanting to be near people will probably prevent them from coming. So for now," she smiles, "let's keep rushing to the Darkness."

AND I FOLLOW her under the glows of the sky, though I do not know the nature of the Darkness any more than she — though I do not know whether I will return here, whether I will ever again move Inward.

I follow her under the glows of the sky, under each color of twisting aurora, under greens and reds and blues that are mixing with the black of the sky and mixing with the stars. And there is much I do not know.

TELLUS LOOKS to me, and the light on her face is the color of the shadows of the stars. “How far is it, to the Sea?”

“I don’t know, exactly,” I say.

“But not so far?”

“Not so far,” I say. “This Land is thinner than yours.”

“I know *that,*” she says, “and this one’s a Constellation. By my names of Lileta and Vei, get that straight.”

I nod.

WE SPEAK little as we walk with silent footsteps. I watch the sway of her hair, as many colors as this aurora, but different ones. In her are the shades of sand, every orange and red. The reds in this Constellation are mostly counterpart to green or faded to pink.

It is still strange, for there to be no ground when I look down.

But I look forward, and occasionally Tellus looks back to me. Her pace matches mine.

There is fog surrounding the auroras in the distance, and it makes them look like a dawn.

WHEN THE true dawn arrives we are slowing, and I follow Tellus' lead in sitting down. Then lying down to rest.

But she says before I sleep: "I was kind of expecting you to ask me how I got the fabric."

"Were you?"

"Well, if you did, I'd tell you."

"I assume you were talking to someone."

"That'd be right," she says. "And I tried to trade it for something, so I said I'd come back later, do something for this person."

I nod and trace the rays of the sun in its rise. I trace the patterns left by residual stars, and perhaps the patterns are constellations.

I do not know if I will be here again.

I CLOSE MY eyes and dream of stars falling inside the stones of my Kingdom. Stars reflected in the water that attaches to them from the river. Stars from here, far away.

When I open my eyes, I see a burst of color that makes me close them again.

I dream the sensation of growing at the same time that I dream of floating.

I dream the question of what Tellus dreams.

I AWAKE AT the start of the next night, and Tellus is looking toward the thickest fog. "That's where the Third Sea is, right?" she asks. "You can tell better than me."

"I think so."

Here the clouds seem to hide the sea. Here all is sky.

When we step forward, I taste salt at the edge of the scent of stars. I nod to Tellus, and we continue.

THE AURORAS flow around us the way clouds flow, and we follow a blue-green one downward. It spirals and in a few steps it catches the light of a blue-tinted star and shifts its color.

The fabric around my body now appears fully green, while Tellus' very skin seems blue. She looks at her hands and she giggles.

When I look to her, she says, "Don't worry, you look nice too."

"And you are the color of the sea."

"Do people come in that color?"

"I am certain they do not."

AND AS WE descend, the taste of stars evaporates while the sea condenses. There is no sand here at the base of the sky, only faint wisps of aurora masked by cloud.

Tellus sets the fabric down and begins to fill it in the way she has been taught, so that it acts like air and floats on water.

When she places it on the Sea, that is what it does.

She motions me into the front of the boat and then follows me in. "To the Fourth," she says.

8

AND ON this Sea, the currents carry us.

Tellus' hand is in the water and a wake is following it. I place a hand in as well and the salt hurts. But I continue to watch the way the water shifts around me.

TELLUS LOOKS back, but her Land is not visible through the mist of the Third Constellation. Neither is mine.

Instead, she looks Outward. In the distance are the tops of trees and nothing taller. Like the First Kingdom in one sense, but not in another. Perhaps not like the Second at all.

For a moment, I imagine she sighs.

I may have only heard distant wind.

WE FLOAT forward, always toward the Fourth Kingdom.
The stars shift above us, and the water pulls us quickly.
For all its quickness, the dawn has past when we arrive.

9

GROUND IS BEFORE us, a rich brown. And water continues in parts, flowing out to the Sea in between the roots of mangroves. It is flat and there is the sound of frogs, there is the sound of wind in leaves, there is the sound of gentle water.

The sun is caught by branches, and shadows cross the ground like lace. In these shadows, fish dart away from birds.

And there are faint colors suspended in the air like scent.

TELLUS REMOVES her shoes and leaves the boat first. She holds her hand out to mine and, when I grab it, she whispers, “May I?” and leans her head in to kiss my wrist.

I let her, and I blush that my first touch on this Kingdom would be this.

But the second touch is the touch of shallow water and the ground beneath, half soil and half sand.

Our hands part, and we stand before this Kingdom.

We see someone from this Kingdom standing before us.

HE IS PERHAPS ten years old, skin the color of clay, hair tousled like the roots of mangroves. He tilts his head at us, but then points at me and asks, "Are you the messiah?"

My eyes shift to Tellus, and she raises her eyebrows at him. He still looks to me, barely blinking.

"Yup," he continues, "your color's right for it. A real First Tributarian. Definite messiah." He pauses, eyes only now beginning to shift. "Should go get someone. Stay right there!"

Then he runs off. A mild reddish trail follows the air behind him.

"Perhaps we should run in the opposite direction," I say.

Tellus shakes her head, her hair moving with the gentleness of a breeze. "Nah," she says, "we should see what happens."

I look to another part of the coastline, and she says, "You agreed to follow my lead."

"I did," I say.

VOICES RISE from behind the trees: "*Potential* messiah, Djoma, let's be cautious."

"Yes, mom."

"From the First Tributary, you say?"

"She's going to unite the Tributaries, swear to the Origin."

I step slightly behind Tellus.

They approach us slowly.

TELLUS LOWERS her posture and says softly, "I hear you're talking of a messiah. Would you explain?"

Her eyes glint, and I expect she will soon speak a new name.

But the newcomers look to me when they answer, "If one has travelled here from the First Tributary, unity between all Tributaries may soon follow." This answer comes in parts, voices trailing away and new voices picking up where they have left.

I look to Tellus, and she darts her eyes to and from me.

I look to the people of this place, and I say, "I travel to the Darkness *only* to travel to the Darkness."

"You will still change the world," a woman says and steps forward, her hair covered and her eyebrows white.

I take a breath, step forward. "That is not what I intend."

THE AIR is still and nothing ripples the shallow water. The sky is open and cloudless. But a soft breeze soon rises, and the woman in front of me smiles. She says, "Then let us feed you, for you have a long way to come."

"The fruits are in season," a younger man says.

The group nods in unison, and I nod back to them.

WE ARE walking under the sun in the cool of these wetlands, and Tellus whispers to me, "Long way to come, not long way to go."

"Explain?" I ask.

"That's what the woman said," she whispers. "She said you had a long way to come. They want things from us."

"They will also feed us."

"We still have to be prepared."

"What name are you, now?" I ask.

She laughs and shakes her head. "I'm talking to just you, so I'm Tellus. You won't get my names that easily."

"You do have a new one, though," I say.

"Yeah."

I ONLY barely notice the color around us, the shades subtle against the light of the sun. And subtle against the shadow.

Where the people here walk, a trail of color follows. Each person a different color. As we walk, the colors fade in the distance, evaporating into the sky,

I look behind me and even to move my arm leaves a streak of green; orange follows even the waves of Tellus' hair.

And when they touch, the colors merge into white

WE TURN toward a large tree, walk into a large hollow formed by the roots. Some voices grow louder; others grow quiet. One looks to me and says, "The Origin connects us all."

Below us, there is sand. In the roots are lanterns, and in the sand are cloth walls and bedding sheets and tables. And the smell of food: warmth and spices and plants.

Tellus taps me on the shoulder; when I look at her, she licks her lips.

"Not worried?" I whisper.

She shrugs. "Not enough to avoid food that smells this good."

THE SAND and shadows beneath our feet here are soft. The warm light from the lanterns catches in the trails of color that swirl around this place, giving hundreds of different subdued glows.

The scent of food is even stronger now that it is being dished into bowls. As this happens, all have gone quiet, so I am quiet as well. I sit where I have been motioned to, and Tellus sits beside me, though I do not recall she was ever suggested to do so.

The food is placed in front of all at the table. Many close their eyes.

And a bell rings.

Eyes open. Several talk, taste their food. I taste it also, and find that it is fish and beans and the juice of citruses. None quite orange though.

Still, it is hearty but soft, so I smile to those who have prepared it.

Then there are mutters: "The woman from the First enjoys what we have made!"

A MAN across the table looks directly to me and says, "I am sorry that we were not more prepared, and so were not able to make anything special for this night."

"It is good," I remind him.

Tellus says, "It is." And with a controlled mouth but wildly grinning eyes, she asks him a question: "So, what's your name?"

"Makahi," he says. "Yours?"

She lets half a sigh escape her before answering, "Kukala."

"So it is," I say, "and I am Theia."

Many of the crowd speak back my name in response.

"Yes," I say, "Theia."

I AM asked no questions, other than if I would like to be shown to my bed.

So Makahi leads me and Tellus up the roots of this tree and into the branches, via a staircase formed of its knots and curves. There are lanterns here too, glowing in the night. We walk across platforms connecting the branches, until we reach an area sheltered from sun and wind by some of the higher branches and the trunk itself. Here there are two large hammocks and several dim but warm lanterns.

"Thank you," Tellus says. I say the same.

When he leaves, I say something else: "Tell me to stop if you need."

So I step to her and kiss her, the taste of oranges stronger than the sound of wind or water. She pulls away only to bite my lip. So I bite hers.

When Tellus does pull away, she smiles and asks, "So what brought this on?"

"I found myself missing the taste of oranges," I say.

IN OUR hammocks, we speak between the stars. We speak because we do not know what we are thought to be.

"They stopped pressing," Tellus says. "Stopped saying so much so often about messiahs."

"And?" I say.

"They're trying subtlety," she says. "They want us to like them so we can be — so *you* can be — this messiah they're wanting."

"I did say we should run."

Tellus laughs then, but says, "It wasn't wrong to stay."

10

THE SUN RISES, and the sky is split between textured clouds and a bright blue sky with only faint wisps of clouds. There are voices louder than bird calls from below us, but they are not loud enough to make out the words.

"Well," Tellus says, "I know *I'd* like some breakfast. But let's still be careful."

So I twist out of my hammock and manage not to fall before I stand. And I walk down the path we were shown, and Tellus follows.

WE ENTER THE same market under the tree as last night, and there are more here than before. They speak loudly, and when they gesture to emphasize an important word, the trails of color that follow movements in this Tributary appear. So around even those now stationary are rings and lines of color.

Even here, the words are difficult to understand because there are so many. Yet I do catch my name often.

Tellus sighs, and I barely hear when she says, "So we can't just have breakfast, huh?"

A WOMAN CATCHES sight of us, and before I can blink we are being moved out of this room and toward another path into the trees. If she speaks, I do not hear amongst all the sound.

The path twists up this tree, and when we turn the first corner, the woman speaks. "We are deeply sorry for what is occurring below. Some disagreements long kept below the surface in our community are beginning to come into the light now when we speak of you."

"Where are you taking us?" I ask.

"There is a private dining room in the top of a nearby tree. I have arranged for fruit and honey to be brought there, as you are surely hungry."

So we loop across branches and lanterns no longer needing their fire in the light of the sun. And we enter a hollow, a room dappled with patterns of light from various holes in the tree.

THE TABLE IN the room is already covered in an array of fruits, with cups of honey on each side, as well as three glasses of water. We sit and the woman who brought us here is still for several moments. When she opens her eyes and eats, I do too.

We eat in silence, and only when the taste of fruit is leaving me do I look to the woman sitting across from us and ask her, "Who are you?"

"I am called Kanakhi," she says.

"It seems you already know our names well," Tellus says.

"Many of us learned them, as we try to learn the names of any traveller," Kanakhi answers.

"Do you call all travelers messiahs?"

Kanakhi smiles. "It is not an insult."

"I agree that it would be quite something to be the light that heralds a new dawn in the world, but you are far overstating what we have actually done," Tellus says, her voice cool and simple. The voice she speaks in when her name is Kukala.

"And for you, Theia?" Kanakhi looks to me.

"Your food is good," I say.

Kanakhi simply replies, "Excellent."

WHEN WE WALK again down the path, the voices have quieted, although there are still signs of discussion. Kanakhi smiles calmly again as we enter the chamber. She says to us: "Do as you will, though there will be meals when the sun is at its peak and when the sun sets."

"Thank you," I say, and begin with Tellus to walk toward the center of the space.

"Thank you?" Tellus asks. "She's playing us."

"I'm *not* stupid," I say. "And you're playing her too."

"All I've done is respond to questions as is reasonable."

"You are trying to deflect her," I say.

"Well," Tellus says, "maybe."

THE VOICES we hear are quiet, and quieter as we walk by, as if they are trying not to be heard. Still, we hear them.

"A messiah with ignorance of her role is in direct contradiction to the entire concept."

"The *only* thing which defines what we call a messiah is one who unites the Tributaries."

"This does not seem to be her plan."

"Volition is not part of the description. She could be a stone cast into the water, and her ripples could be the unified world."

"Or they could be those of a fish flapping about in the water!"

"Are you claiming meaninglessness to one from the First Tributary isolated at the center of the world leaving her prison?"

"It is an insult to the Origin to call any Tributary a prison. The Origin connects us all."

"You understand what I meant."

WE APPROACH the exit. A different conversation is whispered to the side of us.

"What does it mean, for a messiah to have a companion?"

"You raise a good point. For instance, it could be possible that her companion is the true messiah."

"Ah, but as far as we know, this companion has never seen the First Tributary."

"If she goes to the Darkness, then all the way back to the center ..."

"That is pure conjecture. All we know is that one who is in truth from the First Tributary is here and intends even to cross the Seventh Sea. The one who crosses the First and Seventh seas, the ones never crossed, is the one who will bring us unity."

"All I mean is, that description may one day fit both."

THE SUN TOUCHES my face as we approach the outside, and I turn to Tellus and ask, “Is this similar to what you heard when among the groups in the Third Constellation?”

“Of course not,” she answers. “I would’ve told you if there was something like this.”

And we reach the outside of the market, and the sun glistens on the water. The trees display paths we barely noticed yesterday and, where there are no sandbars, roots extend high enough above the surface of the water to be walked on like roads.

So we walk on one such root, like a road.

LEAVES IN THE water make it green, and forms swim underneath: fish and large reptiles and even snakes. In the distance, a fisherman catches a crab.

Unwanted salt from the trees rains sometimes when the wind blows, the crystals catching light in the air. And elsewhere there are people discussing with fervor how I will unite the world — they are speaking of origins and messiahs. Even Tellus had suggested a dawn, when talking to Kanakhi.

The water ripples like ocean currents when a caiman looks briefly above the surface before returning below. Tellus looks to me as if she intends to speak, but she does not. If she is Tellus any more than she is Kukala or any other name.

Were this the Third Constellation, I would walk another path. Were this the Second Land, I would taste the ground. Were this the First Kingdom, I would make the climb to the meadow, even without permission.

Instead I say: "We will sleep, and we will eat, until of their own volition we are taken across the Fourth Sea."

"Oh, *you're* giving orders now?" Tellus asks.

"It's a good plan."

"You might be right," she says.

11

AND ONE night in her sleep Tellus speaks a name. She says, "I must be Henle now, passive." And she mumbles against it, she mumbles, "But-" Cuts herself off with, "It is still my name, so I will use it."

And her words cut out into sleep, and I remember her quiet when she told me she was Henle, I remember the meaning of that name. And still I let the starlight filter in through my eyelids. I let myself wait.

WE EAT CRAB and mango, and as it dissolves in my mouth I hear a man mutter to himself. He says, "The messiah would have perhaps preferred to visit a village that engaged her more."

Another says, "She appreciates us. All is well."

I catch a smile on Kanakhi's face. I also catch that she eats at the head of the table every day and night, and all here listen when she speaks. She is the leader of this place, though she never told us.

And Tellus is Henle as she eats quietly, looking and not speaking. Her hat casting shadows over her eyes.

BUT WHEN WE are outside, in between trees as the sun is halfway down the sky, she says, loud, "I couldn't just stand by, so I learned what I could about the Origin."

"And?"

"The Fourth Tributary believes that all life, even that of animals and plants, has a common origin — that long ago our ancestors were too small to see, and our connection to that time still remains between us. That this connection can think and guide us, like a person."

"It believes, then, that the world was once only one Kingdom," I say.

"They call that the River, from which everything we know now is a Tributary."

I nod.

The birds are singing, but Tellus is far from it. She grabs my hand and looks me in the eye and says, "I can't just do this, Theia. I do not want my Land to be the same as this place."

"It won't be. Just as no one in your Land will ever learn all your names, even though that is certainly the goal of many."

THE NIGHT rises and we finish plates of chicken, but as we turn to leave, Kanakhi says the simple words, "I have an announcement."

All quiet, and she continues: "There are boats gathering on the channel," she looks to me, "the place in all our Tributary where the water is most open. Shall we send one to join them?"

"This is for the messiah and her companion, I assume?" one man says.

"We will be bringing them on this boat, yes," Kanakhi says. "A few others, too. I suggest you decide among yourselves five people who would like to accompany those two and I. We will leave in an hour."

KANAKHI LEAVES a bright white trail as she walks toward the water, where a boat already waits. We follow her.

Tellus whispers: "So perhaps you were right, and they will simply bring us across the Fourth themselves. Though maybe they won't."

"They will bring us across," I say.

"If you want me to not interfere, that's fine," Tellus says. "But before we leave, I *will* learn about these trails we leave when we walk."

I nod.

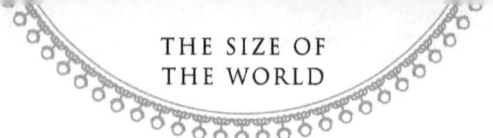

THOUGH THE brightest of stars has already set, we set sail and the man who guides the ship never once falters. And though there is a lower deck where we should sleep, neither Tellus nor I go there. Instead, we stay above and watch the stars through the trees, watch the water blacker than the sky. We feel the wind against our skin.

We do not talk. Instead, we only wait.

12

WE DO NOT sleep until we reach the other boats. Neither does the night.

The dawn is just now a hint in the sky as we see shapes before us, shapes of other boats connected together the way the trees are connected together. Boats like a floating city.

I descend to the lower deck and, exhausted, I sleep.

I dream that I climb the mountain that is my Kingdom. I pass the forests just above the Sea, and I hear waterfalls and streams. I climb the rocks and see the meadow, higher than trees can grow, the air cold and clear to breathe. I reach the staircase etched in the center of the mountain and climb past the winds and snow to the seat of the King himself.

And the King speaks and tells me that he will crown me for my journey across the Seas. And I refuse.

AND ALL I am aware of is the wind in my hair. It twists it sharply. It pulls.

Past my eyelids, it is light but quiet. And I open my eyes.

My hair is still pulled and twisted, played with. But there is also warmth that touches my head. And I see not the wind, but Tellus next to me.

"Stop," I say.

She pouts. "But this is payback for you setting the plans when we agreed I would."

"That was days ago," I say.

"I'm patient."

BEFORE I CAN sit up and brush her hands away, I hear footsteps coming down the stairs to us. Tellus quickly postures herself again as Henle; I look to the location of the sound.

Kanakhi walks to us. “I assume you slept well?” she asks.

“I did,” Tellus says.

“Good,” Kanakhi says. “I was about to walk to one of the larger boats for breakfast.”

“We will follow,” I say.

THE BOATS ARE wood, all reddish brown, but some more sun-stained or mud-stained than others. We walk across a plank to one next to our own.

This one is also nearly empty. One passenger who remains is also making his way across another plank to another ship, the same one we are heading to.

And the sun is bright against the patterns in the wood. And against the ripples the boats cast in the water.

AT A TABLE in the lower deck of a large boat we are quietly sipping water that tastes like hibiscus. And in front of each of us are large papayas filled with a coconut milk and duck stew.

Below us I faintly hear the sound of lapping water. A bell rings, and I sip the stew and the bits of papaya that fall into it.

Some speak. "Nice Messiah you've brought, Kanakhi."

"I am sorry for my brother's rudeness; we are very pleased to meet you."

"May luck and the Origin be with you as you approach the Darkness."

And then we finish eating, and there are so many who speak that I can barely hear.

Until a man clears his throat and all the noise ends. "May the leaders of each contingent introduce themselves one at a time?"

And they do.

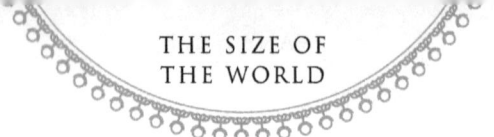

"I AM CALLED Phora, and to know what you are called and that what you are called is Theia is a great honor. Like many here, I truly believe you can be the one to unite the Tributaries. To my knowledge, there has never been anyone more qualified to do so. Thank you for coming here, and thank you for being soon to leave here, moving Outward, toward the Darkness."

I nod and say, "Thank you."

"I AM KUHILI, and I would urge you to go as fast as possible. News of your travel may be meaningless to the other Tributaries until you have done exactly what you set out to do."

Another coughs.

"I know you think differently, Celengu, but you will have a turn to speak when I am done. And having urged speed, I *am* done."

I nod and say, "Thank you."

"I AM THE Celengu who was mentioned before, and I think you go too fast. You must meet with more people! Tell them what you are doing. Tell them what it means! The Tributaries will *never,*" he glances at Kuhuli, "be made whole unless they know to work with you, unless they realize through you just what is at stake."

Tellus takes a sharp breath, and then is silent.

I nod and say, "Thank you."

"I AM CALLED Niwa, and I think it is improper to give advice to one as great as you."

I refrain from coughing.

She continues, "It is proper to give thanks though, so I shall. I give thanks to your very existence, Theia, and that I have had a chance to meet you."

I nod and say, "Thank you."

"I AM LANU, and though I will be called a heretic, I believe in honesty, so I will say this. I do not believe you to be the Messiah. From what I have heard from Kanakhi, you have not set out on a quest to unite the Tributaries, but rather to see them. Perhaps your making this journey will prepare the waters for a future journey made for the purpose we have been waiting for, but only time will tell that, and I am surely too old now to see it myself."

I nod and say, "Thank you."

"I AM DJUNA, but I doubt you care who I am. What you should care about is this: If you do unite the tributaries, it will not be at the moment you first emerge from the darkness. Am I understood? What my fellow leaders have forgotten is that change is a long process, even if it is a change which is meant to be. You will have to slowly build up relations between the Tributaries, using your prestige as grounds to begin. Only that will ever produce results."

I nod and say, "Thank you."

"I AM KIVHUKO, and I will perhaps be called a greater heretic than Lanu. As many in my village are already aware, I do not believe in a Messiah. I wish for unity as we all do, but it is only the acts of societies as a whole that will bring us there. And who can say exactly what the world will be like on that glorious day?

I will say this about you: perhaps at the end of your journey, you will have a better idea as to the answer to that question than I."

I nod and say, "Thank you."

"I AM CALLED Kanakhi, and of course you have already met me. Because I brought you to this gathering, it is important to affirm that I do believe in you, Theia. That is all."

I nod and say, "Thank you."

AND THE LAST, the one who called the meeting, speaks.

"I am called Djakinu, and my thoughts have already been swayed by a correspondent in the Seventh Tributary. For simplicity, I will read the words of her most recent letter, because I believe she can speak not only for herself, but for the good of all of us.

"'I expect you Fourth Tributary people will miss the point entirely. I'd like to remind you that these newcomers' journey is to the Darkness, which even my people fear.

"That they do this is a miracle greater than that of your messiah, and I hope your gathering will not hinder them.'

"With that I announce that the boats shall begin heading Outward — now."

AND WE STAND at the edge of the top deck of the largest ship as we pass through the waters, faster than some of the birds that fly from the trees. If I do not focus my eyes, the trees we pass blur into a green like what I would see if I moved my hand past my eyes.

We are not alone, as there is a man near us who also looks out from the edge. When he smiles, though not looking at us, a glint appears in Tellus' eye and she says, "I'll ask him."

SHE WALKS TO him and says, “Watching the trees go by?”

“Something like that,” he says.

“Hm,” Tellus says. “Not sure yet if you’re the kind to answer questions, so do you mind if I ask one?”

He doesn’t look at her, but he says, “Not at all.”

“The trails which follow us here,” she says, “what are they?” And an aura of orange hovers near her tilting head.

“Those,” he says. “They have been referred to as strings which connect us to our common Origin. Or reminders of where we have come from.”

“They can’t reach as far as where I come from,” she says.

“I know,” he says.

“Not very strong, then.”

“Strong enough to bring you here.”

Then Tellus laughs and says, “Oh, don’t get any ideas,” and walks back to me.

"AND WHAT NAME were you just now?" I ask.

"Not one you've learned yet."

"And what would it take," I say, "to learn it?"

"I'd probably have to play with your hair a lot," she says.

I sit down and wave her over, the wave green. "Then do it, I demand you."

I am looking at the trees so I do not see her, but I feel her fingers in my hair, on my head. Intermittently following the string woven there, though not moving it. Her touch is warm, the wind cold.

I close my eyes.

And do not think of ivy, do not think of mountains. Only of this wind and the orange light around my head.

And the name "Loka," which Tellus whispers into my ear.

AND THE TREES are thinning, the sea close. The sun has moved across the sky, the night has fallen and faded, and the sun moves again.

And we sip ginger tea after a meal of fish and mango, and Kanakhi across from us looks to me. She nods her head and says, "May I talk to the both of you?"

So we follow her across decks, the ripples in the water below thinning as the roots thin.

WE SIT IN another lower deck, and Kanakhi smiles and says, "So."

"We are near to the sea," I say.

"Yes," Kanakhi says, "which is important." That part spoken as half a question. "Perhaps more important than anything else."

"Certainly to you," I say.

"More to you." And she looks to Tellus also. "I recall you speaking more, once."

Tellus bites her lip, so I say instead, "I do *not* recall how much you know of her Land."

"Enough," she says.

"Enough to know I play games but not enough to know that sometimes I get bored of them," Tellus says. "Because that would require knowing about me, not just my Land."

"Of course," she says. "And you would have to know about me to know that I am not offended by your games, only curious how they will end."

"A direct statement, from you," Tellus notes.

"Someone had to be."

13

"BUT NOW we enter the Sea," Kanakhi continues, no white trailing around her. "Some will say it is better that you never knew yourself to be the Messiah," she says, looking at me.

"One is already saying it," Tellus notes.

AND ON THE Sea the sun still moves, though it touches only the waves and these boats. When it begins to set, we gather again. There are no trails. There are no falling stars. There are no changing names. Or certainty.

And people say in quiet voices, "It's like I can barely see when I move." Or, "Where did they go?"

But Djakinu says, louder than the rest: "You are all terribly weak."

And Tellus laughs.

SO WHEN we walk to our room to sleep on the Fourth Sea, Tellus stops before the stairs. "To our success at crossing the Seas!" she says.

And she holds her palm in the air, and softly I slap mine to hers.

And the boats rush across the Sea.

14

I WALK TO the upper deck, and though it is day the sky is near dark as night, and it flashes with lightning. The thunder is loud, and there are voices in the thunder, voices like shouts.

And mountains, sharp mountains darker than even the sky.

I take a breath, and the air is wet though there is not yet rain. And there is a pause in the thunder, a pause in the voices. And then.

And then there is rain, and the thunder starts again and the rain is louder, the rain which already has made me as wet as if I had fallen into the sea. But not wet with Sea, wet with this Kingdom, this Land — whatever exactly it is.

The rain is sharp.

AND FROM somewhere one from the Fourth Tributary shouts also, at me and Tellus. Kanakhi? She leads us to another boat, a small one.

We step on it, and the water of the Sea rocks in the force of the rain, in the force of the wind now starting to blow. I get in, and then Tellus does, and we row toward the shore.

And the wind carries the voices, and I can almost catch the words.

IT IS HARD to see when we land for all the water in my eyes and lashes, but we walk out of the boat.

And the wet sand sticks to our legs.

And I look up, my eyes too blurred with rain to see, like being underwater. The flashes of lightning still visible through it.

And then, it quiets. The flashes become less common. The rain lessens so that it is possible for me to see a figure now walking across the sand and into a small house. And to notice the multiple houses built here in an imperfect circle around a center where several trees and large rocks stand. Some of the houses stone and some wood.

Since I can see, almost, I look to Tellus and I nod.

I WALK TO the house that the figure I saw entered. And I knock on the door, the sound muffled against the damp wood.

Still, the door opens. Before me is a man, his skin dark as night and his hair even blacker, straight and ending lower than his chest.

"What happened?" I ask.

He answers in a hoarse whisper. "The yelling? We don't take kindly to when the Fourth 'Tributary' comes here." He pauses. "But it doesn't look like that's where you're from."

"It isn't," I say. "I am from the First Kingdom."

"Nice," he says.

Tellus raises her eyebrows at him.

"*Would* be more impressive if you came alone." He steps out of the house. "But this is a strange place to talk."

And so he closes his door and walks to the center in the now-soft rain. He leans against a somewhat thin but apparently strong tree, and we stand near him.

"SO," THIS MAN says, "do you know what the Fourth would do to us if we actually let them sail to our beaches?"

"Ahh," Tellus says.

"They have," I pause to find the words, "tried to 'unify' with you before?"

"They've suggested," he says. Then he walks a few steps to a large, twisting black rock and punches it, shattering the top of it with just his hand. He then walks to me and places a piece of it in my hand. "Feel this when it's broken," he says.

And I touch its edge and begin to bleed.

"Exactly," he says. "Now feel the larger piece of obsidian this came from, the unbroken part."

I do, and it is smooth.

"Boring, right?" He walks back to the tree and leans against it with something similar to a smile. "Unity is pointless. So," he continues, "I don't know why you're here. You're not from the Fourth, but you came on one of their ships, and if you're part of their goals I will have to stop you from going any further."

"THAT WON'T be necessary," I say.

"Oh?"

"I was born in the center of the world, and my goal is to journey to the very edge, into the Darkness. I am not doing this for change in the world, although I would not fear change. I am not doing this for power, although I will not deny the power I will gain. I am not doing this for knowledge, not in the way one might assume.

"For the knowledge I do seek is more observation than absolute truth. And I do not seek it to create change or power, as I hope I have already made clear. I seek it to make it part of myself. And that is all."

His smile is an answer.

THOUGH TELLUS HAS more to ask him. "So you don't get along with the Fourth Tributary," she says.

"We certainly don't," he says. "They seem to want to take us over. Although of course I do not speak for everyone in the Fifth Range — it would be so like the Fourth of me if I claimed I did."

And just now a woman I had not noticed walking past takes steps closer to us and says, "For instance, I'm pretty sure they'd like it just as much if *we* took *them* over."

"See?" he says.

"A question," I say. "Which she," I look to Tellus, "would probably prefer asking. What is your name?"

"Lun," he says.

"And I'm Akhi, and I find this conversation interesting."

"Which is an easy way to end a conversation," Tellus says.

So Akhi shrugs and walks away.

"Huh," Tellus says. "Anyway, Lun, when we were escorted by your enemies, we lost track of our own raft. Where should we go on the other side of the Range to get a boat so we can cross the Fifth Sea?"

Lun shrugs. "For that, you'd want to see a cartographer."

SO WE WALK closer to a ridge of the black mountains as the rain begins to stop entirely. And on that ridge, there is another house.

Lun tells us, "There are multiple towns on the Fifth Sea that should have boats. We trade with the Sixth sometimes, giving them shaper tools in exchange for more durable ones." Then he walks to the house and knocks.

And the door opens, and the person standing there is much older than Lun, though their hair, grown just past their chin, is still pure black.

"I've found some people who need a map," Lun says.

"Don't be so smug," the person says. "We all know that the Fourthers landed some people just now."

"But these are not *from* the Fourth, nor are they working for them. Don't be a wet leaf, Kealon."

"Don't be clay, Lun," Kealon mutters, not angry. And then says: "Where do they need to go?"

GAPS APPEAR IN the clouds as we sit and wait for Kealon to complete our map. The sun shines in places, in patches of ground that stand out against the grey.

And then the door opens again, and Kealon walks to me directly and hands me the map.

On the map are symbols in blue and a path drawn in teal. Some of the symbols seem to be mountains, others seem to be not mountains. On two of the corners of the map, the Fourth and Fifth Seas seem to be marked. And the trail sometimes goes above a mountain and sometimes not.

Perhaps Kealon sees the look on my face, and they say, "Hey, I pride myself on giving out only the fastest paths around."

I look to the map again, and then to Kealon. I am not sure how many mountains they want us to climb.

"Not the *easiest*," they continue.

"Thank you very much," Tellus says, and Kealon leaves us.

Lun laughs.

AND WE LOOK at the map as Lun walks us toward the way out of the town, a somewhat hidden path in between the bases of two mountains.

"This is definitely readable," Tellus says.

"Oh?" I say.

"Yeah, we walk between a bunch of mountains and avoid the one that grew a crab, then we walk up a river and up some mountains, take a stairway down …"

"Those are stairs?"

"Think so. Anyway, then we walk as straight as we can through the triangles and a couple of trees, and we will find our boat having a conversation with a swirl."

"That swirl," Lun says, "is a symbol that indicates a town. You were right enough about everything else though."

"*Enough*?" Tellus asks.

"It's *your* journey, I don't have to tell you anything," he says, and shrugs. "Even though you're not going alone."

WE WALK TO the narrowest part of the path, edged by obsidian on either side. Before we pass through and leave Lun, Tellus asks him, “Why does it matter so much if we’re alone?”

Lun shakes his head and says, “It’s hardly *difficult* to travel with a … girlfriend, right? In fact, it’s so easy, I’d be surprised if you discovered anything at all.”

And now Tellus shakes her head at him, but smiles. “Sometimes, parts of us are only visible near other people.”

And together we take a step deeper into the Fifth Range.

15

AND WHEN the clouds part and the sun shines against the obsidian, it is reflected back with all the brightness of starlight.

And Tellus laughs when we are paces away, and she says, "He never asked me my name. I never had to tell him."

"And what would you have told him?"

"What I'll tell the next town, assuming I have to." She looks to me with half a pout. "Theia, it means more when each name is first known by a *different* person."

I nod.

"Though, you *are* perhaps a different person than you were when you first became Theia."

And the wind blows strong through this small valley.

AND EVEN PAST the valley there are mountains, some in the distance and some closer.

"I'm glad," Tellus says, "that you were as direct as you were today. You should try talking like that to me sometime."

"Should I?"

"Oh yes," she says, and turns back to me, smiling, sunbeams falling through her hair. "It's an order."

UNDER OUR FEET, there's pebbles and smoothed obsidian. And I say: "Well, is there something you would especially like to know?"

"Hmm," Tellus says. "It's obvious, but how about how you feel — about me?" And she giggles.

She looks to me then, though I don't blush.

"You know I didn't want you to come at first."

She pouts. "Yeah?"

"You came anyway though, and you're different in different lights, different days. You are willing to look in places I won't, like conversations. All while tasting like oranges."

"How open, for you." She smiles. "That's more what you see than what you feel though, but I'll take it.

As for me, you are the most solid ground I've ever seen. In your certainty, I think I can see some of the core of your being. Now and always. Theia."

"MAY I KISS you?" I ask.

"Please."

And I do, and she is the brightness of orange, like always. So I pull away and say, "Change your name, so I can taste the rest of you."

"Without even being politely asked?" she asks with a teasing smile.

I give a similar smile in response. "As long as you want it, it's an order."

AND EACH OF her names, one by one, is a slightly different taste. Some subtle like mist. Others shining.

Lileta. Vei. Sayeh. Henle. Ulania. Senna. Sesa. Kukala. Loka.

The taste of her names in my mouth is the same as the taste of her. The same as the taste of me thinking of them.

And when I pull away the last time, though her smile is peaceful, she grabs on to my hand and starts leading me down the path.

AND IN THE distance, over the mountains, the sky is again thick clouds. And we pass by them, mountain and mountain, some close and some far. Hills in between.

Above us the sun still shines, but as we walk we reach further into the clouds, until all the light is behind us and caught in Tellus' hat.

And we cross hills and hills, some covered in grass, and others bare rocks.

AND AS SOON as we walk down from the hills, we notice roofs of houses in the distance, notice also that both the greys and the blues in the sky are darker now. Closer to night.

Tellus smiles. "It's been a long day. Let's sleep here."

"We could go farther," I say.

"I remember," Tellus says, "that in the Third Constellation, I gave you five of my names in exchange for you letting me choose how fast we go through each Land, and it sure seemed like you thought those names were worth it *earlier*-"

"Shh," I say, but agree.

SO WE WALK into the village, Tellus ahead of me. Some who are walking about — watching the first stars, leaving toward the mountains, going between houses — look at us. But not all. Not even many.

"Lun was right," Tellus says. "Two traveling together really is boring to them." So she walks faster ahead of me and waves at them. "Hello Fifth Range!" she shouts, "Any inns open?"

One who was looking at us earlier shrugs, another nods slightly. Tellus walks to the one who nodded and says, "Can you point me in the right direction?"

"It's a little bit that way," they say, pointing.

Tellus walks that direction and I follow, and when we reach the stone-carved building with the word *inn* above its door, she knocks.

A MAN OPENS the door. "Hello?"

"Hello," Tellus says, "may me and my *girlfriend,*" she looks directly at me and I think I blush, "have a room here?"

"You mean one bed," I say.

"Is that alright?" Tellus asks.

The man who owns the inn rolls his eyes. "Your couples' whatever really doesn't matter to me, there's only one room open anyway. With one bed. You want it or not?"

"Yes," we both say.

"And payment?" Tellus asks.

"Just a story," he says.

SO WE SIT at a table across from him to tell a story. Tellus and I look to each other for a moment. And then I start talking.

"Once, when I was ten, the guardian of the 32° stream caught me carving the rock there. I used another piece of stone against the stone, and it worked half the time. I thought she would be angry. The stone didn't need to be carved; the patterns in my blood deemed me at birth one well fit for fishing the 32° stream.

"Instead my guardian smiled. She took me then to an upstream waterfall — one I'd already seen, though I didn't tell her — and showed me the way the rocks there had worn with age, how their patterns were like the ones I'd carved.

"We looked at the patterns until she asked me to tell her if there was something else I'd rather do, another area of the Kingdom where I'd be better working. I almost told her I didn't know.

"But I did know, and I said so. I said I would cross the seven Seas and see the Darkness."

THE MAN SMILES and nods. "A strange story to my ears, but a fine payment. I'll show you to your room."

So he walks us to the door of our room, and as I begin to open the door, he speaks.

"I might like to know your name," he says, "since more stories may one day be told about you."

"Theia," I say. "My name is Theia."

AND IN OUR room, I lie in the bed together with Tellus, the light fading as the night outside gets darker. And she whispers to me, "Say my names again."

"May I know them all first?" I ask.

"The ones you *know*," she says.

"Alright, if you would like me to tell you which part of yourself to be again, I will gladly-"

"No, this time I'm telling *you* to tell me to-"

"Senna."

And she calms, and I say all of her names, the ten I know.

"Theia," she says.

"Hm?"

"Theia." And pauses. "Theia."

She is saying my name ten times.

"Theia."

And I sleep.

16

THE NIGHT IS still in the sky when we leave. As she walks across the grass, Tellus waves at the houses. Two or three who walk around, awake, wave back.

The mountains are clearly visible against the stars, jagged and deep black. We walk in silence and watch our steps until the dawn.

AND AS SOON as the dawn arrives we reach a river in a shallow valley, glowing now softly in the dawn's blue light. All the land shadowed but not too dark to see. And the river flows down from a mountain, a mountain which is ahead of us on the path the map shows. The river, too, is on the map; the path suggests we follow it.

So we walk the gentle slope into the valley and follow this river for a while. Then we see ahead high and sharp rocks on either side of the river, too jagged to walk.

So we step down into the river. There are rocks all the way down it, and I stand on one of these rocks, walk onto another. Tellus walks in the river, the river shallow enough to reach only her knees.

And the rocks are slippery from the water, but not entirely smoothed by it. So I walk upriver step by step. Carefully.

And when easier, I cross a shallow part of the river, with Tellus. Then, I feel water. Otherwise, I feel only the wind and the brightening sky.

THE SUN IS still not high enough to warm our skin when we've gone up all the river to its source, a spring surrounded by crystals. I dip my hand into it, drink the water, and it is sweet.

But to our side there is a staircase in the edge of the mountain. Seeming to lead all the way to the top.

"Not the easiest path," Tellus says. Kealon's words.

"Though the fastest," I say.

"So I hear."

We begin up the mountain path, the sun behind this mountain, us in shade, silhouetted against a sky now pale blue.

And behind us is half the Range, the river we walked, the towns. And beyond that, the Fourth Sea we have already crossed.

The dark of the mountain blocks us from seeing the Fifth Sea.

WE REACH A peak, but we see the path leads beyond this peak and to the next. I take a deep breath.

"Actually, it's strange," Tellus says.

"Hm?"

"Exploring alone is a value here, right? It seems like difficult explorations are, too. But this path is already carved."

"Perhaps not the hardest path either."

"So it seems," she says.

AND THE SUN above us. A peak, another peak. So much of this Range in our sight. And the Fifth Sea ahead of us. And even a hint of color beyond that, the Sixth Kingdom.

In that direction, the sky is darker.

The Darkness, which was once my only goal.

THE SUN IS now behind us as we leave the mountains, down a staircase. Now I can understand how the land before us compares to the map. Ahead is a field specked with something rising from the ground. Something that seems like rock or crystal. Not far from that, there's a town. And the Sea.

And a Kingdom past that, and a Sea, a Kingdom, a Sea. That is all that is left.

WE REACH THE field. And Tellus points at what rises from the ground around us and says, "You get two of my names if that's not obsidian."

"Sounds good," I say.

And we walk toward one of the crystals, clouds forming behind us. It is taller than a person, and it is black.

So I walk to it and touch it. Most of it is smooth but an edge is sharp.

"It's obsidian," Tellus says.

But parts of it gleam white.

"Not entirely," I say. "These seem to be diamonds embedded in it." I turn to her.

"So you get one name," she says.

I walk to her. "And what should that name be?"

TELLUS' EYES SPARK, and she grins when she says, "Keha." And then: "The one who danced until dawn."

So she kisses me, and this name is bright the way the stars are.

But when she pulls away she looks to the side and then back to me, and she says to me, "I know this isn't a question that can be asked, but I want to ask it anyway."

"What is the question?"

"Do you know who I am?"

"I KNOW THE way some of your names taste on my lips," I say.

Tellus looks down. It is not enough for her. A moment passes, and she breathes deeply. Then looks back to me, into my eyes. "*You*, Theia, you're the weight of rock, but not held down, not by anything. Like a thousand stones rushing across the world."

I do not know what change comes over my eyes, and I smile.

"You can see me," I state, "but not yourself."

She nods.

"Tellus," I say, "I cannot state exactly who you are."

She looks away.

"But, what I have seen of who you are …" I smile.

A PAUSE. And she smiles back.

"I followed you in hopes that I could learn to see myself like I see you," Tellus says. "But that wasn't the only reason."

"Then follow me again. Walk to me. And," I say with a smile, "tell me to stop if you need."

And I lean against the crystal as Tellus bites her lip, still looking into my eyes. Walking forward, one step at a time.

"And you tell me too," she says, "if *you* need."

AND WHEN SHE's next to me, I whisper, only just loud enough to hear, "Kiss me."

Already she is leaning to me in her attempt to hear. So then leans in further. Her lips against mine, the bright taste of orange.

Until I break away and ask, "Would you like to be held?"

"Yes."

And I ask, "How close?"

"Very."

So in that moment I grasp her, tightly. And my mouth against her ear, I remind her, "If you need."

And I spin around, turning her to stand against the crystal. And I press her shoulders to it. I look into her eyes, look to see a sign of fear or dislike. But there is none, and she has not told me to stop.

So I slowly bring my head toward hers, giving her time to speak.

She only smiles.

And then wraps her arms around me, underneath mine. And as I press her against the crystal she presses her fingernails into my skin, moves them across me in arcs.

BUT I SAY, “I do need,” and withdraw my hands from her shoulders.

Tellus moves around to the side of me, a few paces away. Sits down. Motions for me to sit.

I look to her, and she is blushing when she asks me, “Too much?”

Maybe I am blushing too. I say, “No. You’re shorter than me. I was standing too strangely.”

And Tellus giggles. “That’s alright.”

And I smile.

“So may I hold your hand?”

“Yes,” I say.

Her hand does move to mine, but then moves to my wrist. The sun-shaped scar on her palm against my skin. She holds my wrist tightly, not quite painfully.

AND SOMEHOW just by touching me she feels like more than all the skies, more than all the Lands.

"Around you," she says, softly, "I feel like the thousand colors of the sky. A thousand colors in one sky, heralding the dawn. Heralding the dawn as she travels through the world."

And she looks to me. My breath caught in my throat.

And a moment passes in the long shadow of the mountains.

Then I ask: "Would you like to be held in a way that doesn't require me to stand strangely?"

She grins and she nods and she moves closer to me and she says, "Tell me to stop if you need."

And that is how it becomes night.

17

IT IS MORNING when we wake. I move slowly out of Tellus' arms and say, "We should continue to the Sea."

Tellus nods. "We should."

And the sun is shining through the pale grass and refracting off the obsidian and the diamond. And there are bright white clouds against a bright blue sky.

I grin.

I ENTER SHADE as we pass under a tree with wide leaves that feather out in all directions. There were trees between the crystals and the Sea, on Kealon's map.

There are trees ahead, but spread apart. Grass in between each one, and sometimes exposed rock also.

We walk ahead.

WE CROSS THE field quickly and now there are houses visible, made of sandstone and slate. The Fifth Sea just beyond them.

Tellus enters the village first, and I follow.

There is a boy wondering around town, and Tellus asks him, "Do you know who has a boat here?" He points Outward, and so we walk that direction.

The house is very near the Fifth Sea. There is a boat tethered next to it, visibly.

"I could have found this without asking," I say.

Tellus' response is to knock on the door.

AND THE DOOR opens to a man, old enough that his hair is white, and he asks, "Who are *you*?"

"I'm Keha," Tellus says.

"Theia," I say.

"From another Range," he says.

"Yes," I say.

Tellus asks, "What could we pay you to use this boat?"

He looks at us blankly for a moment. I look to Tellus, and she shrugs. Then the man says: "Oh, the boat out there? That's my old one; when I'm done making the next, I'll be retiring it."

"Any chance that you're done making the next basically now?" Tellus asks.

"What would you pay to have me act as if it is?"

"Information, of course."

"I prefer to trade in material."

"Isn't the Fourth Tributary your enemy?"

"At times."

"Well."

"I see."

AND SO THEY talk, Tellus explaining to him all she knows about the Fourth Tributary, until we may have the boat. Then the man looks at Tellus and at me, and speaks.

"There aren't many places to disembark in the Sixth Range. We are close to one of those places, which is why I have a boat. It's a few degrees Clockwise from here — a beach by a cave. You can cross through that into the Range itself, which is much better than trying to climb the cliffs."

"I thought the *Fifth* was the one with cliffs," Tellus says.

"We'll see," I say.

18

AND SO WE are on the Sea. There is fog above the sea, but we can see rock rising in the distance.

"Two with cliffs, huh?" Tellus asks.

"He calls it cliffs because he is from the Fifth Range, and the Fifth Range has cliffs."

"So you're guessing at others' thoughts now?"

I look to her. "Not like you."

"Not like me, true."

AND ON THE sea the sky passes slowly through afternoon. The sun shines, though only dully, and even the smell of salt feels faint.

We row forward, and occasionally I place my hand in the water and again watch its trails.

THE SKY GROWS orange, and although it is a subtle orange, it shines in Tellus' lips.

I smile when I look at her, because I know what she tastes like, behind those lips.

19

AND THE stars are bright when we land on the shores of the Sixth. What it is exactly, if not a Kingdom or Land, I do not know.

I do know that there are only two Seas past this, and then the Darkness.

So I smile as I step on the sand and look to find it red and rough, as the rocks barring almost all ways into the Sixth are.

"So, the question is, are these cliffs?" Tellus says.

I shrug and nod my head toward the cave.

"Pleasure to obey your command," she says, teasing.

And follows me into the cave.

THE ANGLES ARE right for the starlight to follow us here, reflecting off walls smoother than those outside. There are formations above and below, stalactites and patterns like the veins of a leaf.

There is water on the ground, and perhaps we are following the shallow offshoot of a river.

"The boat," I say. And quickly go to grab it.

THE GROUND IS slick enough that the boat is not hard to pull behind me, and there is a smooth path here that fits it well.

Tellus tilts her head at me, so I say, “I think there is a river.”

And the light is brighter ahead, the cave ending.

There is a river.

AND IT IS a wide river with wide banks, because this is a canyon that stretches perhaps from Sea to Sea. A tall canyon also, with a few scrub-like trees on its walls. The water perfectly clear.

The light of the brightest star shines straight through the water, the water clear enough that I can see a glint in a fish's eye.

I TRAIL THE boat down the offshoot of the river as it begins to merge with the river itself. When I am halfway there and the water is to my knees, I turn to Tellus and say, "Get in."

She walks to me and the ground beneath her is sepia with veins of red. The rock remains solid even in the water, and there is no clay.

She steps into the boat as she whispers, "Tell me to stop if you need." I have a second to smile before she grabs my wrists and pulls me into the boat.

The water is shallow, but we remain afloat. The brightest star overhead.

SO WE ROW through the river of this canyon.

Soon the river turns downhill, moving quickly. I put the oar back in the boat and let the river move us.

I watch the stars above.

Then notice the rhythm of Tellus' breath. She is sleeping. Softly I hold her hand, return my eyes to the waters in front of me, and smile.

SHE SPEAKS BEFORE I realize she has woken. “I was wondering some things about your Kingdom.”

“Such as?”

“In the Fifth Range, you talked about a guardian and a place where you were sent to work. What about your parents?”

I chuckle. “I lived with them,” I say, “but during the day I went to train with the guardian of the 32º stream. And no, I am not telling you her name.”

Tellus pouts.

“My Kingdom was not bad,” I say, “but I had to cross the Seas.”

I WAKE NO longer moving. The boat now on shore. I do not see Tellus, but I assume she's not far. So I watch shadows cross the small plants. I watch the water glisten.

Tellus returns with fruit larger than apples. "Found these on some trees in a ravine," she says.

I take a bite, and it tastes like the ripeness of hundreds of different fruits layered together.

"YOU HAVE not met anyone," I say.

"No," she says, "not yet. But," and she smiles.

"But what?"

"But I found something, and I'm going to make you go see. You ready to follow me?"

I am done eating.

She catches my half nod and says, "Good."

So she leads me to the boat, and we cross the river, then land the boat and begin to walk.

THE SUNLIGHT is on the layers of the canyon walls as we walk, farther from the bank. The grass below our feet bright against the reds of this place.

And part of the canyon turns, into something that is halfway to being a cave. And its rock is shaped into buildings. Like part of the wall itself.

"See?" Tellus says.

It is fully quiet; all I hear is the sound of the river. "There's no one here."

"Yeah." She walks closer to the structures. "Let's look inside," she says, flashing me a smile.

WE WALK TO a door of a building, or what is likely a door. The cracks between it and the surrounding wall are barely visible. Tellus knocks; there is no response. "Nothing happened when I knocked earlier either," she says.

She then pushes against the door. It does not open. "Unfriendly," Tellus says.

"Maybe it doesn't like unknown Second Landers barging in?"

"Oh, you think *you'll* be able to push this open?"

"At least I'm from a place with rock."

Tellus glares at me, but half-smiles also. "Do you even remember my Land? There was rock …"

"Not this kind."

"Your Kingdom wouldn't have this kind either."

I shrug.

"So," Tellus says, "maybe we should be looking for a key."

But I notice an inscription near the door, to its right side. The ridges in the rock read: "Only time will tell."

"THIS PLACE thinks it can beat me, with its cryptic games," Tellus says. "But it forgets I am from the Second Land. We live and die by our cryptic games."

I walk toward the inscription and touch it. The message only barely protrudes from the wall.

"Unfortunately," Tellus says, stretching out the word so that I will look at her, "one part of its meaning is clear. We're not figuring this out today."

"So we head forward."

"Unless we see something that looks like the right kind of key, then we'll come back." She looks to me for a moment. "Not complaining?"

"The river follows the circle of this kingdom. We don't get farther from the Darkness whether we move Clockwise or Counter."

AS WE WALK back to our boat, there is birdsong, and there is wind in leaves. Some of the ground is solid rock, some is just pebbles.

Then the water begins, and there is our boat.

I take a step into the front of the boat. Tellus' hand is on her hip as she looks at me. I tilt my head toward the back of the boat. She sighs, loudly, to be sure I hear, and gets in behind me.

And I begin pushing us through the water, down the river. The sun moving across the sky above us.

20

WHEN NIGHT falls, a sunset-like glow remains on one of the canyon walls just in front of us. Then I hear the voices and know it is a fire.

I look to Tellus, and she gives me a smile, knowing we will stop by the fire no matter what I want. So I nod to her and pull the boat over.

THOSE WHO are at the fire have skin the reddish-brown of much of the rock in the canyon walls and hair just a shade darker and redder. They look to us for several moments before one stands up.

The one who stood, a man, takes another moment before saying, "Who might you be, who walk this path?"

"Theia of the the First Kingdom," I say.

Tellus seems shocked but smiling that I spoke first, and says, "And I'll be called Sesa. Of the Second Land."

"Hm. Few travel in the way you are doing," says the man.

"Toward the Darkness?" I ask.

"Yes, and so alone."

"I exist," Tellus reminds him.

"Still, just two. Of course, you are from another Route, and I am familiar with how the Fifth Route conducts itself."

"As are we," I say.

"But all that aside, we are enjoying a freshly-cooked deer and are willing to accommodate two more."

"Hospitable," Tellus says.

THE DEER IS warm and rich, but while eating it we are asked questions.

The first one is, “How long have you been in this Route?” It is not asked by the one who spoke earlier, but by another.

“A day,” Tellus says. But the one who asked the question was looking at me.

Tellus’ answer is accepted, although another mutters, “Just a day …”

“Is there something we should know?” Tellus asks.

“Only that this Route is hardly something one can experience in a day; even those who’ve been here for thirty years barely know anything yet,” an old woman says.

“It’s true that we came upon a door here with the inscription, ‘Only time will tell’,” Tellus says.

Sitting next to the old woman, a middle-aged person with white-streaked hair, neither feminine nor masculine, smirks.

"IF WE DARE generalize," says the man who first spoke to us.

I look up when he speaks.

"If we do that," he repeats, "then you should know that we of this Route appreciate travel and what is learned from it. And, although there is more than you can yet know that you've never seen, you have also seen things we have not."

"You're asking for us to tell a story," says Tellus.

"Perhaps," he says, and around him children murmur in assent.

"I'm sure I can manage that," Tellus says.

AND BEGINS: "The Second Land is change."

But I say: "The First Kingdom is stone."

"Stone and forests," Tellus says, "from what I hear."

"It is a mountain."

"And you came down it and crossed the First Sea, and so on."

"Yes. I walked down the stream that it would have one day been my duty to fish, I walked through the forest down to the First Sea, and I crossed it."

"To my Land," Tellus says.

"Yes. With different colors than mine."

"Not many oranges where you come from," Tellus notes with a smile.

"HER LAND," I say to those who listen, "is orange and red and yellow, the colors of the sands. And it is sand, but also water."

"Water you can both drink and stand on."

"I found Sesa there."

"But most in my Land," says Tellus, "spend their time in the cities, where power changes like the sands. I preferred the sands."

"And another city's gate?"

"Shush."

"ANYWAY," Tellus says with a cough, "we crossed the Second Sea and made it to the Third Constellation."

"The Third Constellation is sky," I say.

"And only sky. People walk on auroras and eat fallen stars," Tellus says. "I can also make a guess about the value they put in freedom, but I'm not from there, so I can't say for sure."

I CONTINUE: "We crossed the Third Sea to the Fourth Tributary, where the people called me messiah."

"Because they think she'll unite the world, which is what they want," Tellus says, looks to the man, and continues, "Not to generalize."

"The Fourth Tributary is sand and shallow water, with large trees growing from both."

"We mostly spent time in trees, or in a ship, when the leader of the town we found decided to escort us to the Fifth Range. They were hospitable, even if they saw Theia as something she does not see herself as."

A PAUSE. "The Fifth Range, however," Tellus continues, "certainly does not like the Fourth Tributary. When we tried to land, the people there, accompanied by thunderstorm, shouted at us as we came to shore, until everyone from the Fourth backed off."

"There is variety in the Fifth Range," I say. "Mountains, yes, but also their rivers and crystals, expanses and forests."

"And weather," Tellus says.

"Yes."

"There they value individual achievement, by my guess," Tellus says. "But as you mentioned earlier, you know that, and that we did not travel alone enough by their standards."

TELLUS PAUSES and looks to the man, to the person with white-streaked hair, to the child paying the most attention. "But you like stories, right? Then let me tell you one I heard back in the Third Constellation, when Theia was being a loner."

"I-"

"You were being a loner. Now, I'm going to tell a story, though it's not my own."

The people of the Sixth Route nod assent.

"I WAS AT a gathering a lot like this one, with various people of the Third Constellation. Then one, a man, who I'd gotten the name of and in doing so had accidentally made it clear that names are power where I'm from — did I mention that? Well, they are, no one has just one name, and to know any of another's names is worth something. So this man, who I can't even bring myself to tell you the name of, *that* is how I am, says: 'We do not seek power as you do. But we do have power, and I can tell you of it, if just to see the look in your eyes.'

"I wouldn't turn that down, and I didn't. So he began a story that started with the words 'In the beginning.'"

"'IN THE BEGINNING,' he said, 'the sky was still spinning. And even in its spinning, stars would fall from the sky: ten a second, more even. Such that nothing was stationary, and all was awash in light.

"'And in all the day the sun was hot as light, and it blocked out all the blue of the heavens with its brilliance. All was white then. And on some days even the waters would join it in its draw. But at night they would always realize their folly, as the sun would never truly care about *them*. And so the waters would fall from the sky without there being a single cloud.

"'And even elsewhere, the sky also spun, and the stars also fell. But only we learned to consume them, instead of fearing their fire and hiding from the colors of the sky.

"'Then one day the sky slowed, and it seemed the world was in place.

"'But some among us know that elsewhere, something else could coalesce. And the sky could change again.'"

TELLUS SITS BACK with a flair of her arms, and in a single movement those who listened each extend an arm to her.

She smiles, the power in the story not obvious and not something she will explain.

21

"YOU MAY AS well know my name," says the man who first spoke to us. "Kararé."

I look to Tellus and see that she smiles.

Kararé looks to the sky, where the stars have moved. "And now it is late," he says. "We have travelled far today, so we will be sleeping."

"We can as well," I say.

He smiles to us.

And so in the way of those around us, Tellus and I lie down directly on the rock, which is soft beneath us.

AND WAKE to the sun. Others wake also; those from this land talk among themselves as they pack their things. Tellus is already awake, standing and conversing with another.

"We will be moving on today," I hear the other say, "until the next place with rooms in the canyon walls."

"We passed by one of those."

"Clockwise or Counter to here?"

"Counter."

"Good, that's the direction we're moving."

"Also where an interesting door was."

AND SO ALL of us begin to walk, mostly on the banks of the river. Tellus walks with the group, but I wade in the shallows, pulling the boat behind me.

The sun is bright on the reds of the river. The rocks beneath the water all shine.

We pass patterns on the walls, small paths of water running down them, ledges, deer on the ledges. One jumps several ledges, all the way to the top.

And the grasses at the top of the canyon catch the sun. Then Tellus' hair does too, and the reds and oranges dyed in it reflect all the sky's light.

THE RIPPLES CAST by the few who walk in the water with me stop. All look at a young man who walks to a part of the canyon wall where a red jewel shines.

A hawk cries out above us.

I walk to Tellus. Her hair still shines with the color of this place, but the shadow cast by her hat leaves her face the color of the Second Land's sands.

"You look great too," she says.

"I-"

"Yes, yes, you were staring at me. But shush. From what I gather, this is an important time in this man's life."

And from several paces away I hear him say, "I last saw this when I was five. The jewel in the rock is real."

Then Tellus says, "See how the older ones smile?"

I do not respond; another does. The one with white-streaked hair. "I can explain my own people's behavior better than your girlfriend, dear. Move over."

Tellus glares at them and lets them approach us, but does not back away.

"SEE," THEY continue, "we walk around the circle of the Route, from one town hidden in the walls to another. Some of our stops are long, and the Route is long, so it takes a while before we see the same place again. No one truly understands the Route, as such, until living at least twenty, maybe thirty years." They smirk.

I nod.

"As I said, you don't understand. But I take it you're aiming to understand something else, hmm?"

"All I am doing," I say, "is traveling to the Darkness at the end of the Seventh Sea."

"Right, right. Call it that." They roll their eyes and continue, "Anyway, you're not understanding this place by passing through, although you'll see another demonstration later today when we get to that door — see, I figured out its meaning just a year ago and have been waiting to return."

Tellus grins.

"But keep your patience until then!" they say.

SHADOWS DRAW across the river as the sun crosses the sky, until at the first emergence of the stars, the door is visible quite close to us.

"A locked place," someone near me mutters. "And one it looks that we'll be able to enter this time."

The person I talked to steps farther from the bank now, to the door. It reads as it did yesterday: *Only time will tell.*

More begin muttering and whispering, and I only now learn the name of the person with the white-streaked hair: Corona.

"Rélra, please come," Corona says.

The person named Rélra, a very elderly woman, steps forward toward Corona.

"Only time will tell," Corona reads. "It's almost too obvious to be solved, as what does tell, other than time? But the fun thing is, time leaves marks that nothing else can. So Rélra, will you please press your incredibly wrinkled hand to this door?"

And she does, and it opens.

ALTHOUGH THERE are rooms to the sides, the door leads directly to a passage, and Corona decides to let all twenty people from their group, as well as me and Tellus, through. Once inside, it is a tunnel, square the way rooms sometimes are, but with the wet walls of caves.

The only light is that of glowing shells in the walls. "The shells of some of the first to emerge in the world," Kararé says.

Except for that and a comment about the low ceiling, no one speaks.

IT IS MINUTES before I catch the gust of air that carries no scent, only a dull and constant sound.

I smile, and know it, but am surprised that my heart beats quickly. I do not speak what I know, but walk faster.

Tellus waves to someone, perhaps everyone, and catches up to me. We are now behind only Corona.

And when we emerge, it is as I thought: we are looking at the Sixth Sea.

"AH," CORONA says. "Well then. I see now where time has brought me." There is a pause as they lean down to collect sand in their hand, and then to let it scatter in the scentless wind.

"Theia, you left your boat behind. You best get it, as we'll be leaving soon."

"I won't argue about you coming with us," Tellus says. "But Theia would want to."

I stay quiet. The words will do little.

But when we turn back, in the dark of the passage, I whisper other words to Tellus and grab her by the wrist.

I SPEAK UNDER the light of shells: "I won't argue either, not for this Sea, but if she will reach the Darkness it will be separately."

"I would will that also, Theia." She draws out my name such that my hand nearly goes limp and pulls herself from my grasp to grab the edge of my shirt, using it to pull me into a kiss.

I break away to whisper, "Tellus." And then: "A name only I know."

"Yes."

"So that you are mine, if you will it."

"Only if you are also mine," she says, purposeful and certain. "Kneel to me if you will, and only then will I say it's true that the name only you know may have power over me."

So I kneel like a stone falls to the earth.

"Now you own me, Theia."

All my body relaxes in the sound of my only name.

MOMENTS PASS before I can say: "But now they are waiting for us."

"Mm," she assents. Then reaches a hand to me: "Do I need to help you up?"

I take her hand.

"You seem — weak, perhaps."

"Something like," I say.

"That . . . did get somewhat carried away," she says. Blushes.

I likely blush too. "I'm sure we will continue another time."

We exit the passage and move to the boat.

"Even before then," Tellus says. "This name of mine, this part of me, will be yours. At all times, I know it's true."

"And you must know also," I say, "that with a word you can be all I see, the size of my world."

"I do," she says. A pause as she grabs the boat and helps me get it on shore. "Now, to the Sixth Sea?"

"To the Sixth Sea."

THE SIZE OF THE WORLD

"THAT TOOK a little longer than I thought," Corona says.

Tellus responds: "Boats are heavy."

22

THE SIXTH SEA is quiet, and waves barely touch the boat. Corona looks at their Route behind them and then at the rest of the sea.

Tellus and I row, step by step.

The stars change across the sky and a gentle wind blows.

"IT'S STRANGE here," Corona eventually says.

"It is," I say.

They say nothing more.

AND THEN WE begin to approach the Seventh Kingdom, and its buildings tower into the sky. I stare at it as we row.

And the sun begins to rise.

There is something just beyond the city, that the sun's light cannot touch. There is something just beyond the city that is purely and completely dark.

The Darkness.

My breath catches in my throat.

23

THERE IS LITTLE sand at the shore of the Seventh, as so much of the ground is other materials. But there is a small place we can drag our boat onto land, and we do.

"This is my cue to leave," Corona says. "You two are interesting, but Theia here at least is stillness-bent on getting on her way, from what I can tell. I'll be sure to find you if you return."

And with that they walk into the Seventh, on the hard ground, between buildings ten times taller than trees, other people all around them.

Above, something rushes past on a strip of metal.

THEN I LOOK directly in front of me, where a man leans against the building. Tall, with red hair and skin the color of wheat fields. When he meets my eyes, he says, "You might want to find a place to tie that boat of yours."

I nod.

"You got rope?"

I shake my head.

"... Well, it should be fine for long enough to get that," he says. "Here, I'll watch over it." He walks to me and outstretches his hand. "Name's Hirtt."

I grab it, but Tellus answers. "Her name is Theia, and you can call me Iwiti."

"Sure," he says. "There's a store on the thirtieth floor of this building that should have rope. Two squares should cover it. Go ahead and have these," he places two strings of metal sculpted into sharp-cornered squares. "You don't look like you're from around here."

SO WE WALK into the building, the room brightly lit. I do not see stairs; instead, there is a place for us to stand as the ground beneath us is brought meters and meters up.

As we are rising, I say to Tellus: "New name?"

"New place," she says. "Different place."

I nod.

And we reach the thirtieth floor, and we step out.

The store is organized like a marketplace. In one of the corners, there are lengths of rope; I choose one. Then Tellus finds the shopkeeper. I walk up to her, place the two squares on her desk, and walk away with the rope

WE RETURN to tie the boat. The buildings are thousands of shades of metallic oranges and greens, half-transparent against the sky through their wide windows. There are no nearby posts in the ground, but there is a raised part of a carving on the building we just exited.

"Well made," Hirtt says. He still stands next to the building.

I look to him.

"Interesting statement," Tellus says.

He shrugs.

Again something rushes past, far above us, on a strip of metal. "What is that?" I ask.

"Just the monorail," Hirtt says. "Although I do hear they don't have them in other Cities."

"The Seventh City," I say.

"Yes, that is where we are?" Hirtt says.

Tellus explains: "Each of what you would call the Seven Cities have different names. I am from the Second Land, and she is from the First Kingdom."

His eyes widen at the mention of the First. "I've heard of a Senator who would like to meet you."

"OH?"

"Apparently Senator Sun is on the record saying something about wanting to bring someone from the First City here. Didn't think she meant anything real, given how it's her."

"Sun," I repeat.

"Yes, that's her name. Her first one, even, she demands to go by it or something."

I look to Tellus. "We heard of her in the Fourth Tributary."

"You … huh. Well, she's a strange, strange woman," Hirtt says.

"WELL, HOW do we meet this Sun?" I ask.

"The Senate's in Amaranth District," says Hirtt, "which is eight stops Counter on the monorail."

I nod.

"You know how to get *to* the monorail?" Hirtt asks.

"I can see it from here. I'm sure I can find the place to get on," I say.

"We could ask for help," Tellus says.

I raise my eyebrows at her. "Would you prefer it?"

"This time?" she asks. Smiles. "No, I think actually I wouldn't."

I look back to Hirtt and nod. "You heard her. We'll find it on our own."

"Good luck," he says.

THE STREETS are crystal cobblestone, the sky clear, the Darkness still visible Outward. We walk between buildings and follow the sun-reflecting path of the monorail.

No building is not tall. Only the shortest are as low as the highest tree I'd seen in the forests at the base of the First Kingdom. And between the buildings are often paths suspended in the sky.

Others walk on the streets between these buildings, entering or exiting through their glass doors.

We turn a corner following the monorail. There are at least one hundred people walking between the four buildings in front of us.

"You should take my hand," says Tellus, "so you don't lose me."

So I do take her hand.

I LOOK TO the bright sky and follow the monorail's path through it. And turn another corner and see some meters away a second path.

"There's more than one," Tellus says. "Which do we ride?"

"The one we've been following," I say. "The other probably runs Clockwise."

And so we follow the first one we saw.

WISPS OF clouds gather in the sky, and on the tops of some buildings, windmills spin. The path of the monorail turns ahead of us and reaches to the top of another building, one without a windmill.

Where the building touches the ground, there is a door. With Tellus behind me, her wrist in my hand, I walk toward it.

Before I reach the doors, they open for me.

THOUGH SOME look at us, we ask no one if the monorail is where I think it is. I walk to the ground that rises, and this time glass walls close around me when I walk in. The light that passes through refracts orange.

And the doors open at the top of the building.

A wind rushes through.

We step onto a field of wheat, growing here meters and meters above the ground. I turn to look over the edge and other roofs have fields also, many of those with windmills. Some are in bloom.

I turn again and see that the monorail does touch this roof. A shaded station is in front of it.

"I'll be there first," Tellus says, and pulls from my grasp. I open my hand, and she runs to the station.

I run too, but am not as fast.

AND THE monorail rushes to us, larger than I had thought, and stops. One walks out; Tellus and I walk in.

The doors close behind us, and we move faster than the wind.

Tellus walks to a window and I follow. There are hundreds of rooftops below us on the thin strip of the city, flowering and blowing in the wind. The sky still bright.

These buildings pass and then the monorail lands on another, and several walk on. And we move again.

I do not know how far Counter we go. But I number the stops until we reach the eighth, and then we step out the door.

THIS ROOFTOP is covered in amaranth, except for the path between the station and the way down. This place is called the Amaranth District — although I do not know where the government building is.

"We might be going to the tallest building," Tellus suggests.

"Or the most ornate," I say.

But I look over the edge and it is the case that one building, more than all others, is tall enough to touch the clouds.

"Do I win something?" Tellus asks.

"You never said you were betting," I say.

"I definitely win something anyway," she says.

"I could tell you the name those of the First Kingdom would call me," I consider.

"Names die, Theia, and dead names are worth nothing," she responds.

And makes me smile.

WE EXIT TO the ground, and this time, I walk to a woman who has a mechanical hand, her red hair tied up in a bun, and ask her, "Is that tall building where the Senate is?"

She turns to me and says, "It is. For the last century, even, since Erith Green decided the old one wasn't grand enough."

"So it was built, not found," I say.

At the same time, Tellus says: "It's large enough to hold more than a government."

"It also holds the history of the government," the woman says.

The woman is about to walk away when Tellus asks, with a gleam in her eye, "What's it called?"

"The Sword of Dawn," she says.

SO WE MAKE our way to the impressively named building that contains this Senator Sun, who has sent letters to those halfway across the world.

The doors open without a touch, as the last ones did.

Several ask where we are going and why, and the look of where we are from is an answer.

AND WE STAND in front of the doors that bear Sun's name. And they are already open.

We step inside.

24

AND SHE says, "Theia, what a pleasure to meet you."

"You know my name," I say.

"I figured that wouldn't surprise you," she says. "Since you knew Djakinu wrote to me, and could easily have guessed that he did so again after he met you."

Tellus gives a small shake of her head. "I am the one who is more likely to play these games."

"It is good that you are also here, as I expected — Kukala? Of course, you do come from the Second Land, so I can't make many assumptions about your name."

"You call it the Second Land," Tellus says. "And not the Second City?"

"I'm not blind," she says. Then stands to face us, her hair faded to light orange mixed with grey, wearing a grey dress that reaches the floor, and with eyes that do not focus on us. "Well, actually I am blind, but you understand what I mean."

"WHY IS IT we matter to you?" I ask.

Sun smiles. "I'm not using you to unite all people across the Seas like the Fourth Tributary would, if that's what you're thinking. In fact, I daresay I'm not using you at all, since the most I have affected you is to inspire you to meet with me, which I'm glad you are doing."

"That is not answering the question," Tellus says.

"Ah, I would have done well in the Second Land, I think," Sun responds.

And Tellus continues to look at her.

"She's looking at you because you still haven't answered," I say.

"Right," Sun says. "Well now. Tell me: how do you find the fear within my people?"

"YOUR PEOPLE build things taller than trees and near as tall as mountains," I say.

"Actually, we do build mountains," Sun says. "We made two a little while back, to catch the rain."

"That is not a sign of fear," I say.

"We do great things in our lifetimes, us of the Seventh City," Sun says. "It used to be called the Seventh Plain, when we still used hang-gliders to trade with the other parts of the world, before we built the skyscrapers."

"But?" Tellus asks.

"But we are close enough to the Darkness to feel it, if we dare, and we do not dare." She pauses. "Had I timed my wording better, I could have asked before saying that, how many of us you think have been there. But now you can guess the answer is zero, or close enough to it."

"Did you?" Tellus asks. "Is that why you're blind?"

"Oh, no, that's because I stared into the sun when I was a child," she says cheerfully.

"We saw a woman with a mechanical hand," Tellus says. "So it seems you should be able to see, were you to want to."

Sun says nothing.

"YOU'VE EXPLAINED nothing," I say.

"I was close to it," Sun says. "And I'll continue getting closer to it, until you eventually do hear my answer."

"You're interested in one who would enter the Darkness without hesitation," Tellus says.

"*Those* who would," I correct, turning to Tellus. "There is also you."

"But always you first," Tellus says to me.

And there is a flicker at the corner of Sun's mouth. "Yes, it is impressive not just that there is one who is not a coward like those around me, but that she came from the First Kingdom, of all places."

"As I have been told," I say. "And told."

"And as you will continue to be told, especially once you return," Sun says.

"YOU MEAN to set her as an example for your people?" Tellus asks.

"I won't be the one setting her," says Sun. "She sets herself just fine."

"I am not doing this for power," I say.

"All the better," Sun says. "Because as it stands, our fear is so great that not only does no one enter the Darkness, but those who perhaps did don't speak of it."

"Sun," Tellus states the name purposefully, "I can't say that isn't because it *is* frightening."

"And what of Theia?" Sun asks.

THERE IS only one answer.

"I am reaching the Darkness tomorrow."

25

SUN NODS. "You are as you have been spoken of." When I do not respond, she continues: "Well, in that case, you will be prepared a fine feast, and an even finer bed. Do all you must before leaving."

I nod, and she walks forward, motions us to step out.

"I look forward to your return," she says.

THE TABLE in the smaller dining hall on the third-to-top floor is covered with a variety of pastries, wines, and dried flowers. Tellus sits down and puts one of the latter in her mouth. "Yes, they're meant to be eaten," she reports.

The man, Sun's secretary, who led us here, laughs and turns to leave. "Sun told me to let you be alone in here, and to tell you that your suite is around the corner." He pause. "Oh, and also, she'll be finding your boat and having it moved to the Outward edge of the City, in preparation for tomorrow."

I nod, and he leaves.

When he does, Tellus comments: "Intense woman."

THE PASTRIES are sweet in my mouth, and the wine is warm in my throat. The flowers are sweet as well, but more subtly. I find I enjoy them.

As we sometimes did in the Fourth Tributary, we eat our meal in silence.

Outside the windows that cover the wall, the sun begins to set in the sky. The carvings in the archways of the wall cast shadows, and the crystals that hang from the ceiling above us cast light.

I take the last sip of my wine and speak to Tellus. "There was something I said we would finish, in the Sixth Route."

Tellus smiles knowingly. "I do seem to remember something like that," she says.

So I stand and she stands with me, and we walk around the corner.

SILK DRAPES surround the bed, itself with silk sheets, and the light from the window is now bluish in the twilight.

I kiss Tellus, but she kisses me harder. She bites my lip and the pain is bright like a star.

We pull away, and I speak to her quietly. "We both know," I say, "to tell each other to stop, if we need."

"And I will remember to do so," she says. Thinks. "Perhaps there should be a name for doing so. Seawater."

"So it will be," I say.

AND WE MOVE to sit on the edge of the bed. "Should I close the drapes?" I ask.

"If you remain standing," Tellus says, "*Theia*." I make it to my feet, but waver before I take a step forward. Then she speaks again, quiet like wind through empty air. "Theia." My heartbeat is slow but loud, and still I stand. I reach my hand to move the curtain-

And she speaks my name slowly enough that I taste her in the sound. I barely breathe before I fall to my knees.

MY EYES CLOSE, and I feel her place her hands in my hair, against my head.

And I say, "Seawater."

SHE REMOVES her hands and walks farther from me. I take several breaths before opening my eyes, and another several before standing and sitting again on the bed.

"What happened?"

I take a moment. "I am not sure. Perhaps it was too much, too quickly."

"Mm," Tellus says. Then: "I'm glad you said it."

"It was a good idea," I say.

"I'll get you some water," she says. "Would you like to talk, when I return?"

I nod.

I SIP THE water, then say, "I know you might feel that the journey hasn't been long enough, but . . ."

"Do they have regular sleep patterns, in the First Kingdom?" Tellus asks.

"Yes," I say.

"The Second Land sometimes has them. But we can and do sleep for a day, if it's been too long," she says.

A pause. "I've crossed six Seas," I say.

"One more than me, and five has been a lot."

Again, a pause. "I like your idea," I say, "of sleeping for a day."

"Alright, I'm ready to do that," she says, takes off her hat, and quickly lies down on the bed.

I curl up near her, not quite touching, but close enough to feel the warmth of her body.

And night falls on all the City, though our window mostly displays the Darkness.

AND DAY RISES, and I stand to draw all the curtains close.
And lay down again, the distant light against my eyes.

WHICH I NEXT open at nightfall. Tellus is not awake yet, so I exit the room and turn the corner to find another feast.

I eat several of the pastries before Tellus follows me, yawning. "So, it's tonight," she says.

"Yes," I say.

And she sits across from me and eats as well.

I STEP OUT the door of the Sword of the Dawn, and a cool wind rushes across me. Tellus steps by my side. She smiles as the wind blows her hair back.

And then we begin to walk forward on the crystal cobblestone.

The Seventh Sea is only half a mile away.

I LOOK TO the stars, seeing them for the first time in the Seventh City. They are bright despite the softly glowing lights on many of the buildings.

And if I look ahead, I see the only thing here that does not glow with light.

THE STREET ENDS right at the beach, as those at the Inward border of the land did. Waves lap across a small amount of sand just past the cobblestone.

On those waves is our boat.

I look to Tellus and step in the boat. She steps behind me.

The oar is here too, so I begin rowing across the Seventh Sea.

I DO NOT know how close we are when Tellus says, "May I hold your hand?"

"Yes," I say.

Her hand, scarred in the pattern of the sun, presses against me. With just one hand I continue rowing, and the boat still moves toward the pure black in front of me.

And even the quiet of the Sea cannot change the feeling of looking straight into the Darkness, as I move to it of my own accord.

26

AND THEN the warmth on my hand is no longer warmth. It is the feel of the scent of orange in a sudden wind, a wind that turns quickly through the desert and is made of light.

It is Tellus. It is her.

And I realize I do not feel my hand at all.

What I feel instead is more like stone at its core. Were stone to be alive. It is certainty, but certainty that can absorb the world the way ivy absorbs sunlight.

And in it is a stone carved at the base of a waterfall.

And in it are the stars reflected in the waters of a sand dune.

And in it is the sunrise seen through a wisp of aurora.

And in it is the scent of food and warmth under the roots of a mangrove.

And in it is a crystal of obsidian, speckled with diamond.

And in it is the wall of a canyon, more shades of red than I can count.

And in it is a field of grass growing higher than the clouds.

In it — in *me*.

I DO NOT see, and I do not hear. There is no scent or taste. And I cannot tell how I hold my body, I cannot tell which way is down. There is no temperature, and I do not feel the air against my skin.

I do not know if I breathe.

But without any of this, I sense the wisp of orange at the edge of me. I sense its patterns moving, seeing itself, like one who waited for dawn throughout the longest night and is glad, so glad, to see it.

AND SIMILARLY there is a stillness in me that all the rest of what I am notes. I am built around it, stable.

This is why I calm to hear my name spoken by one who understands it.

And now I feel that name, nestled around the stillness, both defining and gaining life from it.

It warms me, though at the same time all of me is cool stone.

There can be both.

AND THROUGH calmness deeper than sleep could hope of, I perceive the twisting of the orange wind, of Tellus, as she configures into thousands of forms. Some are names I recognize, ways of moving I saw in her eyes when she told me those names. Many are not. And the way she opens, like opening her eyes to the new sun, perhaps means that some are names even she did not know.

Though it was I who intended to cross the seven Seas into the Darkness, the nature of it is the very thing she wanted.

A set of colors like warmth passes between us, and with all my self I am happy for her.

SO I REMAIN in my stillness and certainty and observe all that has become part of me. Perhaps etched into me, or perhaps held like a precious gem. Both.

Everything my eyes have been open to see has made it here.

And much more will make it, still.

Like a wave of water passing over me, like a wave that is also fire, I know that always, there will be more moments to capture within me.

And the stillness at the core of my heart whispers back: always.

SO I WAIT for Tellus to see all that she has wanted to see. This is not difficult: the solidity throughout me feels good, and feeling it I understand with absolute certainty now, why Tellus loves me.

And also I understand, why I love her.

She *is* the colors of one thousand dawns, bright in ways both easy and difficult to see. And if she worried that there was not enough consistent about her, she knows now that she is without a doubt her, the same way one would not confuse the wind with a flower or with a lake.

No matter in what patterns that wind moves.

THEN I FEEL her look to me. And grasp tighter onto my hand, sending hundreds of lights through me. And choose to turn.

Of course, I cannot feel that we turn. Nor can I tell if we row or walk. But the decision has been made, and though I cannot feel that we move, I feel in both of us that we will to.

I AM LOOKING into her eyes when I next see, and she is weeping — but they are happy tears, and she is smiling.

I feel her hand as warmth again, although I remember what else it also is. And am sure that I am smiling too.

All I can think to say is, "Tellus."

And all she can respond is, "Theia."

And because I do not know all her other names, I kiss her. And just as I taste like ivy, she tastes like orange.

ACKNOWLEDGEMENTS

ALEISHA, who was my companion throughout the writing of this book. She was always ready to read excerpts and get excited about them, and had probably more confidence in my writing than anything else about me.

ANYONE who read this when I asked them to beta it.

RACHEL ROSE MITCHELL, who was an incredibly helpful resource in the first stages of figuring out how anything about self-publishing worked.

MY EDITOR, Mary Stanfield
(at tautologyauthorservices.com).

MY COVER DESIGNER, Agata Broncel
(at bukovero.com).

MY INTERIOR DESIGNER, Colleen Sheehan
(at wdrbookdesign.com).

And anyone who listened to all my screaming about the process of actually getting this thing out there, thank you guys.

About the Author

IVANA SKYE was born in Boulder, Colorado, though regrettably does not currently live there. Instead, lately she's been splitting her time between Portland, Oregon and Honolulu, Hawai'i in the process of gaining a BA in Linguistics, which she may or may not ever use. This is her first published book, though there are many other writings in her past, most of which should never be spoken of … but are spoken of to friends anyway, just for the amusement of it.

You can find her at ivanaskye.com.

www.ingramcontent.com/pod-product-compliance
Lightning Source LLC
Chambersburg PA
CBHW030320200626
46816CB00006BA/1862
* 9 7 8 0 9 9 7 8 5 4 4 9 7 *